RANDOM
HOUSE
LARGE
PRINT

A Common Life

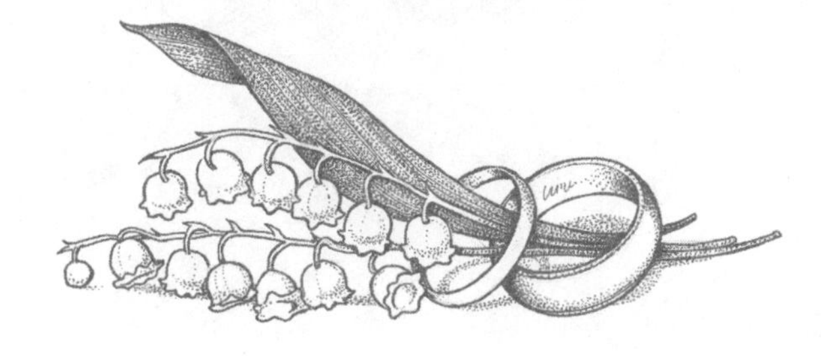

THE MITFORD YEARS

A Common Life

The Wedding Story

JAN KARON

RANDOM HOUSE
LARGE PRINT

Illustrations by Laura Hartman Maestro

 Published in the United States of America by Random House Large Print in association with Viking, New York, and simultaneously in Canada by Random House of Canada Limited, Toronto. Distributed by Random House, Inc., New York.

The Library of Congress Cataloging-in-Publication

Karon, Jan, 1937–
A common life / by Jan Karon.
p. cm.
"Published in association with Viking."

ISBN: 0-375-72814-7 (lg. Print)
1. Mitford (N.C. : Imaginary place)—Fiction. 2. City and town life—Fiction. 3. North Carolina—Fiction.
4. Weddings—Fiction.
5. Large type books. I. Title.

PS2561.A678 C62001b
813'.54—dc21 00-062715
www.randomlargeprint.com

FIRST LARGE PRINT PAPERBACK EDITION

This Large Print Edition published in accord with the standards of the N.A.V.H.

For my much-appreciated
nieces and nephews,
with love

David Craig, Jennifer Craig,
Lisa Knaack, Courtney Setzer, Monica Setzer,
Randy Setzer, and Taja Setzer

Give them wisdom and devotion in the ordering of their common life, that each may be to the other a strength in need, a counselor in perplexity, a comfort in sorrow, and a companion in joy.

Amen.

—*The Book of Common Prayer*

R

Contents

Acknowledgments

Warm thanks to Viking Penguin Chairman Susan Petersen Kennedy; my agent, Liz Darhansoff; my editor, Carolyn Carlson; Paul Halley; Ruth Bush; Kay Auten; Betty Cox; Bishop Keith Ackerman; Father Charles L. Holt; Father Terry Sweeney; Harvey Karon; Martha J. Marcus; Gail Mayes; James Harris Podgers; Betty Pitts, and in the late Hayden Pitts.

Special thanks to Father James Harris, a faithful friend to Mitford; to Victoria magazine for excerpts from Mitford fiction that appeared in its pages; and to the lovely Carolyn Clement, our own Hessie Mayhew, who gathered and arranged the wedding flowers which are captured in pastels by Donna Kae Nelson for the jacket of this book.

A Common Life

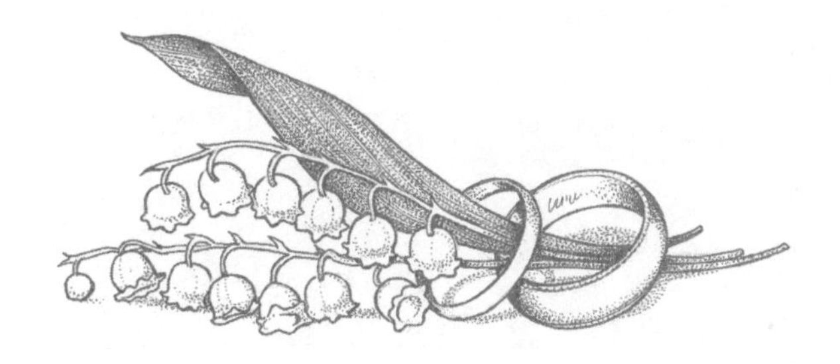

CHAPTER ONE

The Proposal

Father Timothy Kavanagh stood at the stone wall on the ridge above Mitford, watching the deepening blush of a late June sunset.

He conceded that it wasn't the worst way to celebrate a birthday, though he'd secretly hoped to celebrate it with Cynthia. For years, he'd tried to fool himself that his birthday meant very little or nothing, and so, if no cards appeared, or cake or presents, that would be fine.

Indeed, there had been no card from Cynthia, though he'd received a stack from his parishioners, and certainly she'd given no promise of cake or candles that definitively pronounced, *This is it, Timothy, the day you appeared on earth, and though I know you don't really care about such things, we're going to celebrate, anyway, because you're impor-*

tant to me. He was deeply ashamed to admit that he'd waited for this from her; in truth, had expected it, hoped for it.

He'd known suffering in his thirty-eight years in the priesthood, though nearly always because of someone else's grief or affliction. Now he suffered for himself, for his maddening inability to let his walls down with her, to cast off his armor and simply and utterly love her. He had pled with God to consume his longing and his love, to cast it out as ashes and let nothing interfere with the fulfillment of the vows he'd made years ago as an ordinand. Why should such a flame as this beat up in him now? He was sixty-two years old, he was beyond loving in the flesh! And yet, as desperately as he'd prayed for his longing to be removed, he craved for it to be satisfied.

He remembered the times she had shut herself away from him, guarding her heart. The loss of her ravishing openness had left him cold as a stone, as if a great cloud had gone over the sun.

What if she were to shut herself away from him once and for all? He paced beside the low stone wall, forgetting the sunset over the valley.

He'd never understood much about his

feelings toward Cynthia, but he knew and understood this: He didn't want to keep teetering on the edge, afraid to step forward, terrified to turn back.

The weight on his chest was palpable; he'd felt it often since she moved next door and into his life. Yet it wasn't there because he loved her, it was there because he was afraid to love her completely.

Perhaps he would always have such a weight; perhaps there was no true liberation in love. And certainly he could not ask her to accept him as he was—flawed and frightened, not knowing.

He sank to his knees by the stone wall, and looked up and opened his mouth to speak, but instead caught his breath sharply.

A great flow of crimson and gold was spilling across the sky like lava, running molten from west to east. He watched, awestruck, as the pyre consumed the blue haze of the firmament and bathed the heavens with a glory that shook and moved him to his very depths.

"Please!" he whispered.

It was then that he felt a sensation of warmth welling in him, a kind of liquid infilling he'd never experienced before. Something in his soul lifted up, as startling as a covey of quail breaking from the underbrush, and his heart acknowledged, suddenly and finally, that his love for her could not, would not be extinguished. He knew at last that no amount of effort, no amount of pleading with God would enable him to sustain any longer the desperate, wounding battle he had launched against loving her.

In a way he couldn't explain, and in the space of the merest instant, he knew he'd come fully awake for the first time in his life.

He also knew that he wanted nothing more than to be with her, at her side, and that after all the wasted months, he couldn't afford to waste another moment. But what if he'd waited too long, come to his senses too late?

He sprang to his feet, as relieved as if he'd shaken off an approaching illness; then, animated by a power not his own, he found himself running.

"There comes a time," his cousin Walter had said, "when there's no turning back."

He felt the motion of his legs and the breeze on his skin and the hammering in his temples, as if he might somehow implode, all of it combusting into a sharp inner flame, a durable fire, a thousand hosannas.

Streaming with sweat, he raced down

Old Church Lane and into the cool green enclosure of Baxter Park, his body as weightless as a glider borne on wings of ether, though his heart was heavy with dread. She could have gone away as she'd done before . . . and this time, she might never come back.

The dark silhouette of the hedge separating the park from Cynthia's house and the rectory appeared far away, another country, a landmark he might never reach.

As he drew closer, he saw that her house was dark, but his own was aglow with light in every window, as if some wonderful thing might be happening.

He bounded through the hedge; she was standing on his stoop. She held the door open, and the light from the kitchen gleamed behind her.

She stood there as if she'd known the very moment he turned into the park and, sensing the urgency of his heart, felt her own compelled to greet it.

He ran up the steps, his chest heaving, as she stepped back and smiled at him. "Happy birthday!" she said.

"I love you, Cynthia!" His lungs seemed to force the declaration onto the night air as if by their own will. He stood with his mouth

open, marveling, while she raised her hand to her cheek in a way that made her appear dubious, somehow, or amused.

Did she think him mad? He felt mad, riotous, he wanted to climb on the roof, baying and whooping—a sixtysomething bachelor priest, mad with love for his next-door neighbor.

He didn't consider the consequences of this wild skidding out of control; it was now or never.

As she backed into the kitchen, he followed. He saw the cake on the breakfast table and the card propped against a vase of flowers, and he fell to one knee beside the table and gathered her hands in his.

"Will you?" he croaked, looking up at her.

"Will I *what,* dearest?"

"You know."

"No, I don't know."

He knew that she knew; why wouldn't she help him with this thing? He was perfectly willing to bring the other knee down if only she would help him.

And why was he crouching here on the linoleum, sweating like a prizefighter, when he might have been dressed in his best suit and doing this in the study, or in the Lord's Chapel garden by the French roses?

He tried to scramble to his feet and run upstairs, where he would take a shower and brush his teeth and get dressed and do this the right way, but his strength failed and he found he couldn't move; he might have been glued to the linoleum, one knee up and one knee down, frozen as a herring.

"Hurry, Timothy!" she said, whispering.

"Will you marry me?"

"Yes! A thousand times yes!"

She was helping him to his feet, and then he was kissing her and she was kissing him back. She drew away and looked at him with a kind of awe; he found her radiance dumbfounding. "I thought you'd never ask," she said.

It was done. He had jumped over the barbed wire.

He buried his face in her hair and held her close and bawled like a baby.

He was a muddle of happiness and confusion, as if his brain had been stirred like so much porridge. He was unable to think straight or put one thought logically after another; he felt the magnitude of the thing he'd done, and knew he should do something to carry through, though he wasn't sure what.

They had sat on his sofa, talking until three in the morning, but not once had they mentioned what they would do today; they had talked only about how they felt and how mindlessly happy and grateful they were that this astonishing benediction should come to them, as a wild bird might come to their outstretched palms.

"To have and to hold," she had murmured.

" 'Til death do us part," he had said, nuzzling her hair.

"And no organizing of church suppers or ironing of fair linens, and positively *nothing* to do with the annual Bane and Blessing."

"Right," he said.

"Ever!" she said.

He hadn't a single rule or regulation to foist upon her; he was chopped liver, he was cooked macaroni; he was dragged into the undertow of the great tsunami of love he'd so long held back.

They had prayed together, at last, and fallen asleep on the sofa, her head on his shoulder, his head against hers, bookends, then waked at five and scrambled to the back door, where Cynthia kissed him and darted through the hedge, devoutly hoping not to be seen.

He'd bounded up the stairs to his room with a vigor that amazed him, murmuring aloud a quote from Wordsworth:

"'Bliss it was in that dawn to be alive, But to be young was very heaven!'"

Bliss, yes, as if he'd suddenly become lighter than air, as if the stone were at last rolled away from the tomb. He thought he might spring upward like a jack-in-the-box. Was any of this familiar to him, had he ever felt it before? Never! Nothing in his supposed love for Peggy Cramer, all those years ago, had prepared him for this.

In a misting summer rain, he headed for the church office at nine o'clock with Barnabas on the red leash.

He should tell Emma, he supposed, who had served him faithfully for nearly fifteen years. And Puny, the best house help a man could ever have, Puny would want to know.

He could see them both, Emma wincing and frowning, then socking him on the arm with approval, and Puny—she would jump up and down and hoot and shout, and great tears would stream down her freckled cheeks. Then she'd go at once and bake a cake of cornbread from which he, due to his blasted diabetes, might have one unbuttered, albeit large, slice.

Aha! And there was Miss Sadie, of course! Wouldn't her eyes sparkle and gleam, and wouldn't she hug his neck for a fare-thee-well?

And wouldn't Louella break out a coconut cake or a chess pie and wouldn't they have a party right there in the kitchen at Fernbank?

On the other hand, wasn't Cynthia supposed to be along when he broke the news to everybody?

He sighed. He was in the very business of life's milestones, including the occasional overseeing of engagements, yet he seemed to have forgotten everything he ever knew—if, indeed, he ever knew anything.

Besides, he wasn't sure he was up for hooting and hollering and being punched in the arm or any of the other stuff that usually came with such tidings.

Then there was J.C. And Mule. And Percy.

Good Lord, he dreaded that encounter like a toothache. All that backslapping and winking and cackling, and the word spreading through the Grill like so much wildfire, and spilling out the door and up Main Street and around the monument to Lew Boyd's Exxon. . . .

He felt his stomach do a kind of dive, as it always did when he took off or landed in a plane.

If Barnabas hadn't suddenly jerked the leash, he would have walked straight into a telephone pole outside the Oxford Antique Shop.

Bottom line, he decided, Dooley Barlowe should be the first to know. And it was clearly right that they tell Dooley together. He was frankly relieved that Dooley had spent the night at Tommy's and hadn't been there to see him skid through the back door and drop to his knee. Not a pretty sight, he was sure of it.

He could just see the face of his thirteen-year-old charge when he heard the news. The boy would flush with embarrassment or relief, or both, then laugh like a hyena. He would very likely exclaim, *Cool!* then race upstairs with a joy that he dare not freely display.

Still, telling anyone at all seemed hot-headed and premature. This was between

Cynthia and himself; it was their secret. It was somehow marvelous that it was yet unknown to anyone else in the world.

At the corner, he stopped at a hemlock to let Barnabas lift his leg, and suddenly knew he couldn't contain the secret any longer, he was full to bursting with it.

"Make it snappy," he said to his dog. "I have something to tell you."

Barnabas did as he was told, and when they crossed the street, the rector of the Chapel of our Lord and Savior paused in front of the church office and said under his breath, "I've just decided . . . that is, Cynthia and I are going to get . . ."

His throat tickled. He coughed. A car passed, and he tried again to tell his dog the good news.

But he couldn't say it.

He couldn't say the *m* word, no matter how hard he tried.

As he opened the office door, he realized with complete clarity where he should begin.

His bishop. Of course. How could he have forgotten he had a bishop, and that such a thing as this thing he was going to do would be of utmost importance to Stuart Cullen?

But, of course, he couldn't call Stuart this morning, because Emma Newland would be sitting at her desk cheek-by-jowl with his own.

He greeted his longtime, part-time secretary as Barnabas collapsed with a sigh onto his rug in the corner.

Desperate to avoid eye contact, he sat down at once and began to scribble something, he knew not what, into his sermon notebook.

Emma stared at him over her half-glasses.

He put his left elbow on the desk and held his head in his hand, as if deeply thoughtful, feeling her hot stare covering him like a cloak.

Blast, he couldn't bear that look. She might have been examining his tonsils or readying him for colon surgery.

"For heaven's sake," he said, swiveling around in his squeaking chair to face the bookcases.

"I'd leave heaven out of this if I were you," she said, sniffing.

"What's that supposed to mean?"

"I mean, I can't imagine heaven wantin' anything to do with you this morning."

Church secretaries had been fired for less, much less, he thought, grinding his teeth. The office was suddenly doing that bizarre thing it sometimes did—it was growing rapidly and infinitely smaller; it was, in fact, becoming the size of a shoe box.

He bolted to his feet and half stood behind his desk, trying to get a deep breath.

"Your collar's too tight," she said.

"How do you know?"

"Your face is red as a beet."

"It's possible that I'm having a heart attack," he snapped.

"I'm telling you it's your collar. Are you wearin' one of those Velcro deals?"

"Yes."

"Let it out a little."

Dadgummit, she was right. He realized he was nearly choking to death. He adjusted the Velcro, disgusted with himself and everybody else.

What had happened to the soft, circumcised heart God had given him only last night? Where had the lighter-than-air spirit of this morning fled? Why was he grumping and grouching when he ought to be leaping and shouting?

Barnabas yawned and rolled on his side.

"I'm getting married!" he blurted uncontrollably. Then he sat down, hard, in his chair.

He would never be able to explain the mysteries surrounding love, only one of which surfaced when he confessed his news to Emma.

By the involuntary utterance of those three amazing words, his frozen Arctic tundra had been transformed into a warm tropical lake. Something in him had actually melted.

In the space of a few moments, he had become jelly. Or possibly custard. Then a foolish smile spread across his face, which seemed destined to remain there for the rest of his life.

When Emma left for the post office, vowing not to say a word to anyone, he prayed at his desk, went to the toilet and did a glucometer check, then positively swaggered to the phone to call his bishop.

Stuart's secretary said he was either in the loo or in a meeting, she wasn't sure which, but she would check and have him call back.

He slumped in the chair, disappointed.

But wait. *Walter!* Of course, he must call Walter and Katherine at once.

The names of those with special interest in his good fortune were being revealed to him, one by one, in the way some are given inspiration for their Christmas card list.

Since Cynthia had never met Walter, his first cousin and only known living relative, he supposed he was on his own for spilling the beans to New Jersey.

"Walter!"

"Cousin! We haven't heard from you in the proverbial coon's age."

"Which phone are you on?" asked the rector.

"The kitchen. Why?"

"Is Katherine there?"

"Just blew in from the nursing home, she's teaching them to finger paint. What's up, old fellow?"

"Tell her to get on the phone in the study."

"Katherine!" bellowed Walter. "Pick up in the study! It's clergy!"

"'Lo, Teds, darling, is that really you?" He could see the tall, thin-as-a-stick Katherine draped over the plaid chaise, with the cordless in one hand and her eternal glass of ginger ale in the other.

"Katherine, Walter," he said. "Are you sitting down?"

"Good heavens, what is it?" asked Walter, clearly alarmed.

"Teds . . . those tests you were going to have weeks ago . . . is it . . . ?"

"Dooley, is it Dooley?" asked Walter. "Or Barnabas? We know how you feel about—"

"I'm getting married," he said.

There! Twice in a row, and already it was getting easier.

The other end of the line erupted into a deafening whoop that could have filled Yankee Stadium. He held the receiver away from his ear, laughing for the first time this morning, as Barnabas leapt from the rug and stood barking furiously at the clamor pouring forth from New Jersey.

When Stuart hadn't called back in twenty minutes, he phoned again and was put through to the bishop's office.

"Stuart? Tim Kavanagh here. Are you sitting down?" He was truly concerned that no one go crashing to the floor in a faint.

"For the first time today, actually! What's up?"

"Remember the woman I once brought to visit you and Martha?" That wasn't what he wanted to say. "When we, ah, gave you the bushel of corn? *Cynthia!* You remember. . . ."

"I remember very well, indeed!"

"Well, you see, it's like this. . . ." He swallowed.

He heard his bishop chuckling. "Like what, Timothy?"

"Like . . ."

He was momentarily frozen again, then the custard triumphed.

". . . we're getting married!"

"Alleluia!" shouted his bishop. *"Alleluia!"*

Tears sprang suddenly to his eyes. He had been friends with his bishop since seminary, had confided his heart to him for years. And now came this greatest confidence, this best and most extraordinary of tidings.

"Martha will be thrilled!" said Stuart, sounding as youthful as a curate. "We'll have you for dinner, we'll have you for tea . . . we'll do it up right! This is the best news I've heard in an eon. Good heavens, man, I thought you'd never screw up your courage. How on earth did it happen?"

"It just came to me that . . . well . . ."

"What came to you?"

"That I didn't want to go on without her, that I couldn't."

"Bingo!" said his bishop.

"I, ah, went down on one knee, couldn't help myself."

"You should have done the full kneel, Timothy, she's a prize, a gem, a pearl above price! You dog, you don't deserve such a one!"

"Amen!" He said it the old Baptist way, with a long *a,* the way he was raised to say it.

"Well, now, thanks be to God, what about a date?" asked Stuart.

"We're thinking September, I know that's a busy month for you, but . . ."

"Let's see, I have my calendar right here." Deep sigh, pondering. "Alas, alack." Stuart's fingers drumming on his desktop. "Good heavens, I'd forgotten about that. Hmmm. Ahh." Tuneless, unconscious humming. "No, certainly not then."

If Stuart couldn't do it, they'd get it done somehow, they were definitely not waiting 'til October. . . .

"Oh, yes, look here! I've got September seventh, how's that? Otherwise, I can squeeze you in on—"

"I'm not much on being squeezed in," said the rector.

"Of course not! Will the seventh work for you, then?"

"We're willing to take whatever you have open."

"Then it's done!"

"Perfect!" said the rector.

"Now," said Stuart, "hang up so I can call Martha."

CHAPTER TWO

The Grill

"You goin' to have babies?" asked Dooley.

"Not if I can help it," said Cynthia.

Searching the boy's face, Father Tim felt sure their news was a go, but wanted to hear Dooley declare it. He put his arm around Dooley's shoulders. "So, buddyroe, what do you think about all this?"

"Cool!" said Dooley.

Hallelujah! Dooley Barlowe had been buffeted by every violent wind imaginable before he came to live at the rectory over two years ago. Abandoned by his father and given by his alcoholic mother to his disabled grandfather, the boy had known only upheaval and change.

"Nothing will change," the rector promised. "You'll keep your same room, everything will flow on as usual. The only difference is, Cynthia will live here . . . instead of there." He gestured toward the little yellow house next door.

"I like her hamburgers better'n yours, anyway."

"Yes, but she doesn't have a clue how to fry baloney the way you like it. That's my little secret." He loved the look of this red-haired, earnest boy he'd come to cherish as a son, loved the rare surprise and delight shining in his eyes. Dooley and Cynthia had gotten on famously from the beginning, and Dooley's stamp of approval was more important than that of any bishop.

Not wishing to waste time gaining ground, Dooley gave Cynthia his most soulful look. "Since I'm goin' off t' 'at ol' school pretty soon, I bet *you'll* let me stay up 'til midnight."

Ah, politics! thought the rector, happily observing the two. They're everywhere.

Both Dooley and Emma had promised to keep mum, but truth be told, they were only human.

Before there was a leak, however unintentional, the news must go in Sunday's pew bulletin, thereby giving his parish the dignity of hearing it in church instead of on the street. As this was Friday, he supposed he should tell the guys at the Grill before they heard it from a parishioner. But would they keep it quiet until Lord's Chapel got the news on Sunday?

Then there was Miss Sadie. She definitely wouldn't like reading it in a pew bulletin.

He went home at eleven, changed hurriedly into his running clothes, and jogged up Old Church Lane with Barnabas.

He had just run down this hill to do the thing that resulted in why he was now running up it. Life was a mystery.

Huffing, he zigged to the left on Church Hill Road. Then he zagged to the right and ran up the driveway instead of cutting through the orchard like a common poacher.

Miss Sadie and Louella were sitting on the porch, fanning and rocking.

Each time he came to Fernbank's front porch, the years automatically rolled away. With these two old friends, he felt twelve, or possibly ten. Fernbank was his fountain of youth.

His heart pounding, he sat on the top step

and panted. Barnabas lay beside him, doing the same.

"Father," said Miss Sadie, "aren't you too old for this running business?"

"Not by a long shot. I do it to keep young, as a matter of fact."

"Pshaw! Too much is made of running up hill and down dale. I've never done such a thing in my life, and I'm coming up on ninety and healthy as a horse."

Louella rocked. "That's right."

"Is that lemonade?" asked Father Tim, eyeing the pitcher on the wicker table.

"Louella, what's happened to our manners?" asked Miss Sadie.

"I don't know, Miss Sadie. I 'spec' we don' get enough comp'ny t' hardly need manners."

Louella put ice in a glass and handed it to Fernbank's mistress, who, ever conserving, poured the glass half full.

He got up and fetched the lemonade from her, wondering what on earth they would think about his announcement. He'd envisioned them as happy about it, but now he wasn't so sure. He drank the lemonade in two gulps and stood on one foot, then the other.

"You itchy," said Louella.

They could read him like a book.

"Miss Sadie, Louella, are you sitting down?"

The two women looked at each other, puzzled.

Of course they were sitting down, how stupid of him to ask such a thing, it had flown out of his mouth. "Joke!" he said feebly.

"Father, why don't *you* sit down? Get in this chair next to me and start rocking!"

He did as he was told. "Yes, ma'am." Eight years old.

"Louella and I like to rock in harmony, you pay a penny if you get off track."

"Who's leading?"

Miss Sadie looked at him as if he were dumb as a gourd.

"Honey, Miss Sadie always lead."

"Here we go," said Miss Sadie, looking bright and expectant. Since her feet barely touched the floor, this would be no small accomplishment.

After a ragged start, they nailed their synchronization, then worked on building momentum. Miss Sadie was flying in that rocker. . . .

Lord knows he couldn't sit around on porches all day like some jackleg priest, he had things to do, people to see, and besides, he was getting married. . . .

"Miss Sadie, Louella, I have great news."

The two women looked at him eagerly, never missing a beat.

"I'm getting married!" he shouted over the roar of six wooden rockers whipping along on aged white pine.

Miss Sadie's feet hit the floor, Louella's feet hit the floor. Their rockers came to a dead stop. His was still going.

"To Miss Cynthia?" asked Louella, who was generally suspicious of good news.

"The very one!" he said, feeling a stab of happiness and pride.

Louella whooped and clapped her hands. "Thank you, Jesus! Thank you, *thank* you, Jesus!"

Miss Sadie dug a handkerchief from the sleeve of her dress and pressed it to her eyes. "This is a happy day, Father. I can't tell you how happy we are for you. Cynthia is the loveliest imaginable lady, so bright and positive, just what you need. I hope you've been on your knees thanking the Lord!"

He had, actually.

Louella was beaming. "Miss Sadie, I'm

goin' t' cut us all some pie." As she opened the screen door to go inside, she turned and said, "An' remember you owe me five dollars!"

They heard Miss Sadie's longtime companion shuffling down the hall in her slippers. "Why, may I ask, do you owe Louella five dollars?"

She looked at him, barely able to conceal her mirth. "Because, Father, I bet five dollars you didn't have it in you to marry that lovely woman!"

Knowing how dear five dollars was to Sadie Baxter, he smiled at his favorite parishioner and said, "I suppose I could say I'm sorry you lost."

She patted his arm fondly. "Actually, Father, your good news declares that we've all won."

He typed it on his aged and finicky Royal manual and passed it to Emma, who would do whatever she did to work it into the bulletin:

> ii publish the banns of marriiage between Cynthiia clary Coppersmiith of the pariish of the Chapel

of our Lord and Saviior and father Tiimothy andrew Kavanagh, rector of thiis pariish. iif any of you know just cause why they may not be joiined together iin Holy Matriimony, you are biidden to declare iit.

Mitford Muse editor J. C. Hogan slammed his overstuffed briefcase onto the seat in the rear booth and thumped down, huffing.

Mule Skinner, local realtor and longtime Grill regular, slid in beside Father Tim.

"So, what are you roughnecks havin' today?" asked Velma, appearing with her order pad.

Mule jerked his thumb toward the rector. "I'm havin' what he's havin'."

"And what might that be?" This was not her favorite booth; at least two of these turkeys could never make up their minds.

"Chicken salad sandwich," said the rector, always prepared, "hold the mayo, and a side of slaw."

"I don't like slaw," said Mule.

"So sue me," said the rector.

"Make it snappy. You want what he's havin' or not?"

"I don't like slaw," Mule repeated. "I'll have what he's havin', except hold the slaw and give me mayo."

Velma pursed her lips. It was definitely time to retire. Some days, she'd rather work a canning line at the kraut factory than come in here and put up with this mess.

"I'll have th' special," said J.C., wiping his perspiring face with a square of paper towel.

"What special?" asked Mule. "I didn't know there was a special."

"Th' sign's plastered all over th' front door," said Velma, thoroughly disgusted. How Mule Skinner ever sold anybody a house was beyond her.

"So what is it?" asked Mule.

"Raw frog's liver on a bed of mashed turnips."

The rector and the editor roared; the realtor did not.

"I don't like turnips," said Mule.

J.C. rolled his eyes. "Just bring 'im th' frog's liver."

"Dadgummit, give me a BLT and get it over with."

"You might try sayin' please," snapped

Velma, who had to talk to some people as if they were children.

"Please," said Mule through clenched teeth.

"White or wheat?" Velma inquired.

"Wheat!" said Mule. "No, make it white."

"Toasted or plain?"

"Ahhh . . ."

"Bring 'im toasted," said J.C.

Velma stomped off and came back with the coffeepot and filled their cups, muttering under her breath.

"What'd she say?" asked Mule.

"You don't want to know," said Father Tim.

He stirred his coffee, though there was nothing in it to stir. Maybe he shouldn't say anything until everyone had eaten lunch and felt . . . happier about life in general. After all, Mule was scowling, and J.C. had his nose stuck in the Wesley newspaper, checking to see if any *Muse* advertisers had defected to the *Telegram*.

He hoped the ensuing discussion wouldn't collapse into a mindless lecture on his advanced age. Age had nothing to do with it, nothing whatever. No one else had bothered to bring it up, and even if they'd thought it, they had the common decency not to mention it.

Then again, why wait to spill the beans? Maybe there was no such thing as the right time with this crowd.

"I've got some great news."

J.C. glanced up and took a sip of coffee. Mule swiveled toward him and looked expectant.

"Cynthia and I are getting married."

The coffee came spewing out of J.C.'s mouth, which was not a pretty sight.

Mule put his hand to his ear. "What's that? I can't always hear out of—"

J.C. wiped his shirtfront with a napkin. "He's gettin' *married.*"

"Don't shout, for heaven's sake!" snapped the rector. He might as well have blared it up and down Main Street from a flatbed truck.

"Who to?" asked Mule.

"Who do you think?" asked J.C., who had apparently appointed himself the rector's official spokesman.

"Cynthia," said Father Tim, wishing to the Lord he'd never mentioned it. "And I have to ask your complete confidence, you're not to tell a soul until it comes out in the pew bulletin on Sunday. I need your word on this," he insisted.

"You want me to swear on th' Bible?" asked Mule.

"No, just promise me. I didn't want you to hear it on the street, I wanted to tell you in person. But I don't want my parish to hear it on the street, either."

"Done," said J.C., shaking hands across the table.

"You've got my word," said Mule.

"Son of a gun. Married." J.C. shook his head. "I thought you had good sense."

"I do have good sense. Look who I'm marrying." His chest actually felt more expansive as he said this.

"Now, that's a fact," agreed J.C. "Cynthia Coppersmith is one fine lady, smart as a whip and good-lookin' into the bar-gain. What she sees in you is a mystery to me."

"You sure about this?" asked Mule. "Is it a done deal?"

"Done deal. We'll be married in September."

Mule scratched his head. "Seems like you're a little . . . *old* for this, seein' it's the first time and all. I mean, sixty-five—"

"Sixty-two," said the rector. "Sixty-*two*."

J.C. looked grim. "I wouldn't get married if somebody gave me a million bucks. *After* taxes."

"You all are a real encouragement, I must say." The rector heard a positive snarl in his voice.

"Hold on," said Mule. "We're glad for you, cross my heart an' hope to die. It just shocked me, is all, I'll get over it. See, I'm used to you th' way you *are*. . . ."

"Right. Emerson said it was a bloomin' inconvenience to have to start seeing somebody in a new light. But here's to you, buddyroe." The editor hoisted his coffee cup as Velma delivered their lunch.

She carried a plate in each hand and one in the crook of her right arm. "Take this offa my arm," she said to Mule. He took it.

She set the other two plates down and stomped off.

"I didn't order this," said Mule.

"That's mine," said J.C., snatching the plate.

"If I'd known that's what you were havin,' I'd of had that. Country-style steak is practically my favorite." Mule gazed with remorse at his sandwich, which featured a dill pickle on the side.

"I don't like pickles, you want my pickle?" he asked the rector, who hadn't felt so generally let down since the choir and the organist got the flu simultaneously and the congregation had to sing a cappella.

It was all rushing by in a blur. He didn't want to lose this moment so quickly. He wanted to savor it, rejoice in it, be thankful in it.

He put on his pajamas and pondered what was happening.

It gladdened him that he wanted to see her at the slightest opportunity; he yearned toward his neighbor as if a magnet had been installed in him on the night of his birthday, attracted to some powerful magnet in her.

How he wished the magnet had been installed sooner. He didn't want to think of the time he'd wasted trying to make up his mind. But no, it hadn't been his mind that was slow to make up, it was his heart. His heart had always pulled away when he felt happiness with her; each time the joy came, he had retreated, filled with the fear of losing himself.

He remembered the dream he'd had when she was in New York, when their letters had helped thaw the frozen winter that kept them apart. He dreamed he was swimming toward her in something like a blue lagoon, when his strength failed and he began to sink, slowly, as if with the weight of stones. He felt the water roaringin and the great, bursting heaviness of his head. He had come awake then, gasping for air and crying out.

Now there was the custard feeling, which would terrify most people if they didn't recognize it for what it was—it was love unhindered.

This, too, took his breath away, but by the grace of God, he was easy with it, not enfeebled or frightened by it.

No wonder he had counseled so many men before their walk down the aisle; the true softening of the heart and spirit toward a woman was usually an alarmingly unfamiliar feeling. How might a man wield a spear and shield, preserve his very life, if he were poured out at her feet like so much pudding?

He turned off the lamp and went to his knees by his bed, praying aloud in the darkened room.

"Father, we bless You and thank You for this miracle, for choosing us to receive it.

"May we treat the love You've given us with gratitude and devotion, humor and astonishment.

"May it be a river of living water to bring delight and encouragement to others, Lord, for we must never hold this rare blessing to ourselves, but pour it out like wine.

"Protect her, Lord, give her courage for whatever lies ahead, and give me, I pray, whatever is required to love her well and steadfastly all the days of our lives."

There was something else, something else to be spoken tonight. He was quiet for a time in the still, dark room where only the sound of his dog's snoring was heard.

Yes. There it was. The old and heavy thing he so often ignored, that needed to be said.

"Father—continue to open me and lay me bare, for I have been selfish and closed, always keeping something back, even from You. Forgive me. . . ."

The clock ticked.

The curtains blew out in a light breeze.

"Through Jesus Christ, our Lord.

"Amen."

CHAPTER THREE

The Fanfare

The tidal wave, the firestorm, the volcanic spew—all the things he'd dreaded had come at last, and all at once.

People were pounding him on the back, kissing him on the cheek, slapping him on the shoulder, pumping his hand. One of his older parishioners, a mite taller than himself, patted his head; another gave him a Cuban cigar, which Barnabas snatched off the kitchen table and ate in the wrapper.

Well-wishers bellowed their felicitations across the street, rang his phone off the hook at home and office, and generally made a commotion over the fact that he had feelings like the rest of the common horde.

Cynthia's phone got a workout, as well. In approximately three days since the news had hit the street, a total of five bridal showers had been booked, not to mention a luncheon at Esther Cunningham's and a tea at at Olivia Harper's. Emma Newland was planning a sit-down dinner with the help of Harold's mother, and the ECW was doing a country club deal.

He was stopped on the street by Mike Stovall, the Presbyterian choirmaster, who offered to throw in sixteen voices for the wedding ceremony, which, including the voices at Lord's Chapel, would jack the total to thirty-seven. "A real tabernacle deal!" enthused the choirmaster. "And tell you what, we'll throw in a trumpet! How's that?"

(He'd hardly known what to do about the Anglicans from Wesley, who offered to throw in a handbell choir.)

Had he agreed to Mike Stovall's ridiculous offer? He didn't think so. He might have mumbled something like "Great idea," which it was, but would Mike take that to mean he'd accepted? Thirty-seven people in the choir would barely leave room for the bride and groom to squeeze to the altar.

His head was swimming, his stomach was churning, his palms were sweating, he felt like . . . a rock star. That heady notion was soon squelched, however, when he was forced to dash to the toilet at the church office and throw up. He flushed three times, trying to disguise the wretched indignity of the whole appalling act.

"Something I ate," he said to Emma, who knew a lame excuse when she heard one. He snatched a book off the shelf and sat with his back to her, numb as a pickled herring.

"I'm sorry," he told Cynthia one evening at the rectory.

"Whatever for?"

"For . . . you know . . . the ruckus, the . . . the *tumul*!"

"But dearest, I love this! There's never been such ado over any of my personal decisions. It's wonderful to me!"

"It is?"

"And can't you see how happy this is making everyone? Sometimes I think it really isn't for us, it's for them!"

"Wrong," he said, taking her hand in his. "It's for us."

"Then please relax and enjoy it, darling. Can't you?"

She looked at him so searchingly, with such a poignant hope, that he was weak with a mixture of shame for his current dilapidation and love for her bright spirit.

"Of course. You're right. I'll try. I promise."

"Please. You see, this will only happen to us once."

There! She'd nailed it. What made him uneasy was that it was happening *to* them; he preferred having some say-so, some . . . *control.*

"Let God be in control," she said, smiling. He was unfailingly astonished that she could read his mind. "After all, He's done a wonderful job so far."

Bingo! The tension flowed out of him like air from a tire.

"Ahhhh," he said, sitting back on the sofa and unsnapping his collar.

The bishop rang him shortly after dawn.

"Timothy! I know you're an early riser. . . ."

"If I wasn't, I am now."

"Martha and I want the two of you to use our old family camp in Maine, it's on a lake, has a boathouse and two canoes, and an absolutely glorious view! We're thrilled about all this, you must say yes, we'll call at once and make sure it's set aside. . . ."

His bishop was gushing like a schoolgirl.

"And wait 'til you hear the loons, Timothy! Mesmerizing! Magical! Our family has gathered at this house for nearly fifty years, it might have been the set of *On Golden Pond*! Trust me, you'll be thrilled, you'll think you've expired and shot straight up!"

"Thanks, Stuart, let me get back to you on that, we haven't really discussed what we're going to do."

"Don't even think about Cancún, Timothy!"

He hadn't once thought of Cancún.

"And get any notion of southern France out of your head . . ."

He hadn't had any such notion in his head.

". . . it's all the rage, southern France, but you'll like Maine far better! It's where Martha and I spent *our* honeymoon, you know."

He hardly knew what to say to all the offers pouring in; Ron Malcom had offered the services of a limousine following the wedding, but he'd declined. Why would they need a limo when they were only going a block and a half to spend their wedding night?

Esther Bolick sat in the den that opened off her kitchen and stared blankly at *Wheel of Fortune;* it was nothing more than flickering images, she didn't give a katy what a five-word definition for *show biz* might be.

She glanced irritably at Gene, who was snoring in his recliner after a supper of fresh lima beans, new potatoes, fried squash, coleslaw, and skillet cornbread. They'd also had green onions the size of her fist, which Gene took a fit over. "Sweet as sugar!" he declared. She had never trusted a man who wouldn't eat onions.

She was thinking that she was happy for Father Kavanagh, happy as can be. But it had been *days* since she heard the good news and not *one word* had anybody said to her about baking the wedding cake. She knew Cynthia was very talented; she could do anything in the world except cross-stitch, so she could probably bake her own cake.

Well, then, that was it, she thought with relief. That was why nobody had said doodley-squat about her famous orange marmalade being the center of attraction at one of the most important weddings in Mitford in . . . maybe *decades.*

On the other hand, why would anybody in their right mind take time to bake their own wedding cake when all they had to do was dial Esther Bolick at 8705?

She had designed that cake over and over in her mind. Considering that the color of the icing was white, she might crown the top with calla lilies. Jena Ivey at Mitford Blossoms could order off for callas in a heartbeat. She'd even thought of scattering edible pearls around on the icing; she'd never used edible pearls before, and hoped people's fillings wouldn't crack out and roll around on the parish hall floor.

She also considered wreathing the base of the cake with real cream-colored roses, plus she'd have icing roses tumbling down the sides—after all, she'd seen a few magazines in her time, she was no hick, she knew what was what in today's cake world. And would she dun the father for all that work? Of course not! Not a red cent, though Lord only knows, what they charged for ingredients these days made highway robbery look law-abiding.

Esther pursed her lips and stared, unseeing, at a spot on the wall.

The thing was, it didn't make a bit of sense for somebody to bake their own wedding cake . . .

. . . so, maybe somebody else had been asked to bake the cake.

The thought made her supper turn to a rock in her digestive system. She balled up her fist and rubbed the place between her ribs, feeling the pain all the way to her heart.

How could they ask anybody else to bake the father's wedding cake? He had raved about her orange marmalade for years, had personally told her it was the best cake he had ever put in his mouth, bar none. *Bar none!* So what if two pieces of it had nearly killed him? It was his own blamed fault for stuffing himself!

And how many orange marmalades had she carried to the doors of the downtrodden, the sick, the elderly, and the flat broke? And how many hundreds of miles had she walked from fridge to oven to sink, getting varicose veins and bad knees, not to mention bunions? Well, then—*how many*?

She remembered the rueful time she baked marmalades the livelong day and finally dragged herself to her electric-powered recliner, where she pressed the button on her remote and tilted back to what Gene called "full sprawl." All she lacked of being dead was the news getting out, when, *blam!* the most violent and sudden storm you'd ever want to see hit square over their house and the power went out. There she was, trapped in that plug-in recliner, clutching a dead remote—with no way to haul herself up and Gene Bolick out to a meeting at the Legion hut.

She recalled the shame of having to pitch herself over the side like a sailor jumping ship; landing on the floor had caused her right leg to turn blue as blazes, then black, then brown, not to mention her hip, which, as she'd told the doctor, had given her sporadical pain ever since. And all that for what? For four orange marmalades to help raise money for a new toilet at the library!

Trembling slightly, Esther picked up the TV remote and surfed to a commercial with a talking dog. She and Gene had never had a dog and never would, they were too much trouble, but she liked dogs. She tried to occupy her mind with dogs so she wouldn't think about a shocking idea that suddenly occurred to her. Her attention wandered, however, and there it was, the bald truth, staring her in the face:

Winnie Ivey!

Winnie Ivey was exactly who they'd turned to for this special, once-in-a-lifetime deal—Winnie Ivey, who was a *commercial* baker; Winnie Ivey, who'd never made just *one* of anything in her life!

She sat bolt upright and tried to get her breath. Commercial flour! Commercial butter! And, for all she knew, powdered eggs.

Her blood ran cold.

"Of all th' dadblame things to do!" she said, kicking one of her shoes across the room.

"What?" Gene raised his head and looked around. "Was that you, dollface?"

"Do you know who they've asked to bake the weddin' cake?"

"What weddin' cake?"

"Why, the father's, of course!"

"Who?" asked Gene, genuinely interested.

"Winnie Ivey."

Gene burped happily. "Well, I'll say."

"You'll say what?" she demanded.

When his wife stood up and leaned over his recliner as she was now doing, he thought she looked ten feet tall. "I'll say that was a dirty, low-down trick not to ask you to bake it!"

There. Gene Bolick knew what side his bread was buttered on.

She was stomping into the kitchen, mad as a hornet, when the phone rang.

"Hallo!" she shouted, ready to knock somebody's head off.

"Esther? This is Cynthia Coppersmith, I'm so glad you're home, I thought you and Gene might have gone bowling tonight. Timothy and I agree we'd like nothing better than to have one of your fabulous three-layer marmalades as our wedding cake. We hope you'll be able to do it, Timothy said we'll pay top dollar!"

Cynthia was astounded to hear Esther Bolick burst into tears, followed by a pause in which there was considerable murmuring and shuffling about.

"Hello!" Gene bawled into the phone. "Esther said tell you she'd love to bake your weddin' cake! And no charge, you tell th' father no charge!"

Now his choir was upset because the crowd from down the street had horned in.

Had he actually agreed to such a plan? He remembered only that Mike had brought it up, nothing more. He called Mike Stovall.

"I believe we talked about your choir joining our choir for—"

"Right! And everything's going great, just great! We've got a couple of ideas for the music—"

"The music, of course, is entirely Richard's domain, Richard's and Cynthia's, so—"

"Well!" Mike Stovall sounded annoyed.

"In any case, given the small quarters of our nave and chancel, I think it might be best to—"

"Oh, we've thought that through, Father, here's the deal. Your choir in the chancel, ours in the rear, what do you think?"

He couldn't think. He needed a job foreman, somebody in a hard hat. . . .

"It *will* be September, you know."

Hessie Mayhew—*Mitford Muse* reporter, Presbyterian mover and shaker, and gifted flower arranger—had come to consult with Cynthia in the rectory living room. As Father Tim served them lemonade and shortbread, he couldn't help but listen. After all, wasn't he a gardener? Wasn't he interested in flowers?

He crept to a corner of the room with a glass of lemonade and appeared to be wholly absorbed in scratching his dog behind the ears.

"And in September," said Hessie, "there's precious little that's worth picking." Hessie had staked her reputation on what she foraged from meadow and pasture, roadside and bank. Her loose, informal bouquets were quite the hit at every spring and summer function, and her knowledge of where the laciest wild carrot bloomed and the showiest hydrangeas grew was both extensive and highly secret. However, as autumn drew on and blooms began to vanish, she hedged her bets—by dashing cold water on her clients' heady expectations, she was usually able to come up with something agreeably breathtaking.

"What does this mean?" asked Cynthia, looking worried.

"It means that what we mostly have to deal with is pods."

"Pods?" His fiancée was aghast.

Hessie shrugged. "Pods, seeds, berries," she said, expanding the list of possibilities. "Unless you'd like *mums.*" Hessie said this word with undisguised derision.

Mums. He noted that the very word made his neighbor blanch.

Cynthia looked his way, imploring, but he did not make eye contact. No, indeed, he would not get in the middle of a discussion about pods and berries, much less mums.

"Pods and berries can be wonderful," Hessie stated, as if she were the full authority, which she was. "Mixed with what's blooming and tied in enormous bunches, they can look very rich hanging on the pew ends. Of course, we'll use wide ribbons, I'd suggest French-wired velvet, possibly in sage and even something the color of the shumake berry." As a bow to tradition, Hessie enjoyed using the mountain pronunciation for sumac.

He stole a glance at Cynthia from the corner of his eye. How had that gone down? She seemed uncertain.

"Why can't we just order dozens of roses and armloads of lilacs and be done with it?"

Hessie sucked in her breath. "Well," she said, "If you want to spend *that* kind of money . . ."

And let the word get out that his bride was a spendthrift? That was Hessie's deeper meaning; he knew Hessie Mayhew like a book. He knew, too, that Hessie considered the ordering of lilacs in September to be something akin to criminal—not only would they cost aroyal fortune, they were *out of season in the mountains*!

"Not to mention," said Hessie, pursing her lips, "they're out of season in the mountains."

"Excuse me for living," said his fiancée. "Anyway, we *don't* want to spend that kind of money." In truth, his bride-to-be had the capability to spend whatever she wished, being a successful children's book author and illustrator. Besides, thought the rector, wasn't it her wedding? Wasn't it their money to spend however they liked? He hunkered down in the chair, anonymous, invisible, less than a speck on the wall.

Cynthia heaved a sigh. "So, Hessie, whatever you think. Sage and burgundy . . . or let's call it claret, shall we? Burgundy sounds so . . . *heavy*. Do you think we should intermix the ribbon colors along the aisle or put sage on one side and claret on the other?"

The color deepened in Hessie's ample cheeks. "Sage for the bride's side and claret for the groom's side, is my opinion!"

"Of course, I don't have any family for the bride's side. Only a nephew who isn't really a nephew, and the last I heard, he was in the Congo."

His heart was touched by the small sadness he heard in her voice, and so, apparently, was Hessie's.

"Oh, but you *do* have family!" Hessie threw her head back, eyes flashing. "The entire parish is your family!"

Cynthia pondered this extravagant remark. "Do you really think so?"

"*Think* so?" boomed Hessie. "I *know* so! Everyone says you're the brightest thing to happen to Lord's Chapel in an *eon,* and you must *not* forget it, my dear!" Mitford's foremost, all-around go-getter patted Cynthia's arm with considerable feeling.

Click! Something wonderful had just taken place. Hessie Mayhew, sensitive to the bone underneath her take-charge manner, had for some reason decided to be his fiancée's shield and buckler from this moment on; and nobody messed with Hessie.

"We'll fill every pew on the bride's side," Hessie predicted. "We'll be falling over ourselves to sit there! It's certainly where *I'm* sitting—no offense, Father."

Cynthia took Hessie's rough hand. "Thank you, Hessie!"

Thank you, Lord, he thought, forsaking his invisibility by bolting from the chair to refill their glasses all around.

"And what," inquired Hessie, "are you planning to do, Father, other than show up?"

Hessie Mayhew was smiling, but he knew she was dead serious. Hessie believed that every man, woman, and child, including the halt and lame, should participate in all parish-wide events to the fullest.

"I'm doing the usual," he said, casting a grin in the direction of his neighbor. "I'm baking a ham!"

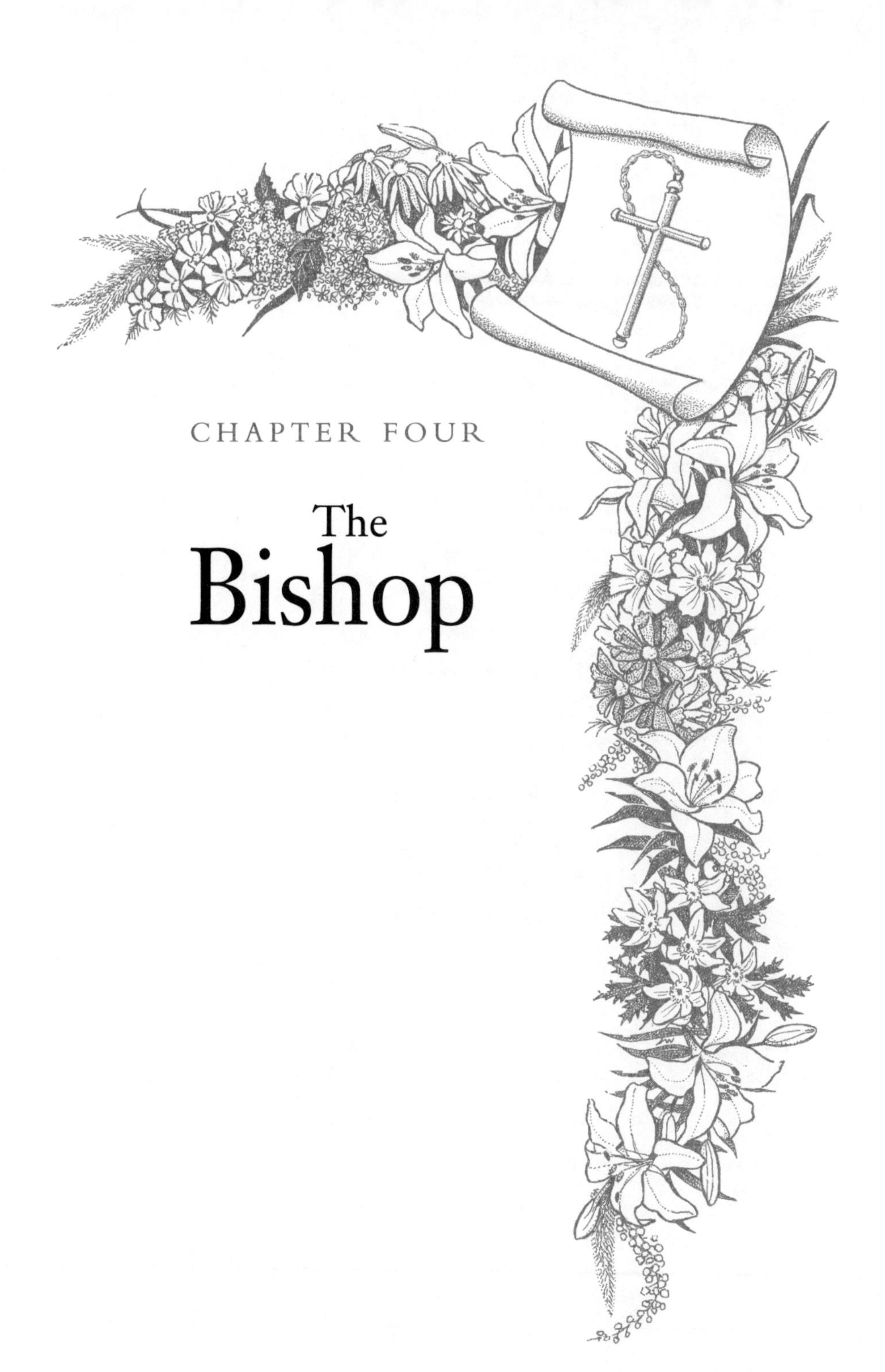

CHAPTER FOUR

The Bishop

"Gone to seed" is how the rector once fondly described his rectory home of more than thirteen years. Puny's eagerness to keep the place fastidious had, he was certain, worn away at least a stratum of walnut on the highboy, a gram or two of wool on the Aubusson, and a millimeter of sterling on the tea service.

She was now feverishly removing another layer from the whole kaboodle, in preparation for any celebration that may be held in the rectory, since, she said, Cynthia's house was too small to cuss a cat, no offense to Violet.

Nearly overcome by the odor of Lemon Pledge, he went to the phone and dialed his neighbor. "Want to bring your notebook and go to the park?"

"I'll race you!" she said.

They sat on the bench and listened for a moment to the birds and a light wind that stirred the leaves in Baxter Park. He kissed her, lingering. She kissed him back, lingering still more. She drew away and fanned herself with the notebook, laughing.

"On to more serious matters!" he exclaimed. "First order of business—pew bulletin or invitations, what do you think?"

"Pew bulletin! That way everyone knows, and those few who aren't in the parish, we'll call. I'll try to reach David, though I can't imagine he'd trek all the way from the Congo to Mitford!"

"Where shall we put Walter and Katherine? Your place or mine?"

"First things first," she said. "We need to know where we're spending our wedding night."

"The rectory?"

"But darling, your bed is so small."

"Yes, but your bed is so *big*." In his view, they could hold a fox hunt on the vast territory she called a bed.

"Draw straws!" she said, leaning from the bench to pluck two tall spears of grass. She fiddled with them a moment, asked him to close his eyes, then presented them in her fist.

"Gambling again," he said.

"Long one, my house, short one, your house."

He drew the short one.

"Rats in a poke!" fumed his neighbor.

"Watch your language, Kavanagh."

"Isn't it a tad early to call me Kavanagh?"

"I'm practicing."

"Anyway, there's your answer. Walter and Katherine spend the night at my house."

"Done!" He checked the topic off his list. "Have you thought any more about flower girls?"

"Amy Larkin and Rebecca Owen!"

"Perfect. Music?"

"Richard and I are just beginning to work on it—let's definitely ask Dooley to sing."

"Splendid. Should have thought of it myself."

"A cappella."

"He doesn't go for a cappella."

"He'll get over it, darling, I promise, and it will be wonderful, a true highlight for everyone. 'O Perfect Love,' what do you think?"

"There won't be a dry eye in the house.

By the way, we're scheduled for the bishop on Wednesday at eleven o'clock."

"What are you wearing?" she asked.

"Oh, something casual. A pink curler in my hair, perhaps."

She swatted his arm over this old joke.

"I love you madly," she said.

"I love you madlier."

"Do not!"

"Do, too!"

"Prove it!"

"I shall. I'm serving you dinner tonight, Puny made chicken and dumplings."

"Chicken and dumplings!" she crowed.

"With fresh lima beans."

"I'm your slave!"

"I'll remember that," he said.

He felt the same age he usually felt at Miss Sadie's house.

Here he was in his bishop's office, seated next to his sweetheart, and only minutes away, they'd be talking about sex. He felt the blood surge to his head, coloring his face like a garden tomato. Though he was the priest, presumably competent to discuss a wide variety of personal issues, it was, in fact, Cynthia who felt perfectly at ease talking about anything to anybody, anytime.

They were currently in the touchy area of Financial, always the leading subject on Stuart's program for premarital counseling. Thus far, they were in good shape, having discussed some days ago what Stuart called his bottom-line on the issue:

Consult with the other about significant purchases, be open about your assets and willing to share equally, and agree on a budget that puts God first.

"And how do you feel, Timothy, about having a wife whose income is significantly greater than your own?"

Blast. Why couldn't Stuart have the discretion to avoid this issue? He and Cynthia had discussed it, but he hadn't been completely candid with her. He hesitated, hating this moment for both of them. "Not good," he said at last.

Cynthia looked at him. Did he see hurt or surprise, or both?

"God brought us together," he said. "He knew what He was doing. And if He doesn't mind the inequity in what I bring to the marriage, then I know I'm not to mind it, either. But—sometimes I do.

"Please understand that I don't resent her

greater assets, not in the least—Cynthia Coppersmith is the hardest-working, most deserving woman I've ever known. The problem, if there is one, is that . . ." He paused. What *was* the problem? Hadn't he pondered this on several sleepless nights?

"The problem," said Cynthia, "is loss of control! Isn't that it, dearest? You've feared a loss of control all along, from the beginning. And now I'm the one who could buy a new car or take us to Spain—"

"I don't want to go to Spain," he said, feeling suddenly vulnerable, close to tears. He also didn't want a new car; he was perfectly happy with the old one.

Stuart smiled.

"If you're all that God wishes you to be in marriage, you will be one flesh. The money must belong to you equally, Timothy. In your heart you must be able to accept it, not as money you've worked for and earned, but as money God means you to have in stewardship with your wife."

Cynthia leaned over and kissed him on the cheek. Tears sprang instantly to his eyes and escaped to the sides of his nose before he could press them with a handkerchief.

"I think," he said, "that I'm overwhelmed on every side. I still can't think why God should give me this tremendous blessing—a gracious and loving soul who comprehends the depths of my own soul completely—and then to add financial resources beyond my wildest dreams . . .

"In truth, money means very little to me. I've lived simply all my life, and can't imagine doing otherwise."

"You've been exceedingly generous to others," said Stuart. "For example, you've poured your personal revenues into the Children's Hospital for years. Now, Timothy, you must allow someone to be generous with you, if she so chooses."

"I so choose!" Cynthia patted the rector's arm.

Relieved, they all had a sip of water from glasses waiting on a tray.

"Another crucial issue," said Stuart, "is in-laws."

"We won't have any!" Cynthia crowed.

Stuart smiled paternally. "In truth, you will."

"We will?"

"According to the Lord's Chapel membership register, there are one hundred and eighty-three of them, which roughly translates to a mere hundred and twenty-five *active* in-laws."

His fiancée appeared vexed, to say the least. "Yes, and there are some who can't bear the sight of me anymore. Everything was just fine until—"

"Until they learned you were getting married," said Stuart. "Then the jealousy flooded in. They were there first—they got his undivided attention for years—now it must be divided."

"Ugh," she said.

"What I hope you'll be able to live with is that his attention to you will also be divided. Like them, you'll have to share your priest. Unlike them, you must also share your beloved, your sweetheart." Stuart looked fondly at Cynthia. "If anyone can do this, you're the one."

"Thank you," she said. "Pray for me."

"Martha and I have prayed for you since the day Timothy brought you to lunch. We both thought you possessed the most extraordinary light, it reflected upon our friend like a beacon. We thank you for that."

The rector noted with a pang of tenderness that his fiancée blushed deeply, something he rarely witnessed.

"I've always felt it takes especially noble character to be a clergy spouse," said Stuart.

"In any case, you and they will soon grow accustomed to sharing him; it's all a process—a matter of time and patience and love. I know you're willing."

"Yes!" she said. "Oh, yes!"

The bishop folded his hands across his lean midsection and gazed at his visitors.

Here it comes, thought the rector.

"Do you pray together?" asked Stuart.

"Yes!" they said in unison.

"Every evening," volunteered Father Tim.

"Excellent! I'm reminded of what our friend Oswald Chambers said, that prayer doesn't fit us for the greater work, prayer is the greater work. Praying together affirms you as one flesh, and, among the endless benefits it bestows, it can greatly enhance your sexual communication."

A patch of light danced upon the worn Persian carpet, reflecting the branches of a dogwood tree outside the window.

"The highest form of prayer is one in which we don't beg for ourselves," said Stuart, "but seek to know what we can do for God. This delights God immensely! As you seek to know what you can do for the other, you will surely receive your own inexpressible delight."

The rector took Cynthia's hand.

"To put it simply, making love confirms your spiritual relationship, and your spiritual relationship will deepen your lovemaking. It all moves in a wondrous circle."

The rector and his neighbor drew a deep breath at precisely the same moment and looked at each other, laughing.

"Now!" said Stuart.

"Now, what?" asked Father Tim.

"Conflict resolution."

"Do we have to?" asked Cynthia.

"Have you had any conflicts?"

The two looked at each other. "His car," she said.

"What about my car?" queried the rector.

"Don't you remember? I said it was a gas guzzler, has rust, and the seat covers look like Puny's dishrags."

"And I said I'm perfectly satisfied with it." There! The bishop wanted conflict, he got conflict. The rector felt his collar suddenly tighten.

"And so," Cynthia told Stuart, "when we drive on the Parkway or visit our bishop, we take my car."

"How do you feel about that?"

She wrinkled her nose. She stared briefly

at the ceiling. She smiled. “I can live with it.”

Stuart chuckled. He had his own opinion of his priest’s car, but far be it from him to comment. “It’s terrific that you’re willing to name the conflict, my dear. This equips us to attack the problem instead of attacking the other person.”

Stuart sat back in his chair. “So, Timothy, how do you feel about driving her car instead of yours?”

“Good!” he said, meaning it. “I can live with it.” He pressed Cynthia’s hand and turned to look at her. She appeared to sparkle in some lovely way he’d never seen before. After his brief moment of righteous indignation, he was custard again.

On the way home in her Mazda, he noticed that she looked at him fondly more than once.

“Sweetie pie,” she murmured, patting his knee.

Sweetie pie! As a kid, he was called Slick; Katherine called him Teds; one and all called him Father. He liked this new appellation best of all. Maybe one day—*maybe*—he'd look into trading his Buick for a new model. But certainly nothing *brand*-new, no; no, indeed.

CHAPTER FIVE

The Joke

He drove to the Wesley mall and looked in the display cases at the jewelry store.

His heart sank like a stone. There was absolutely nothing that measured up to the fire and sparkle, the snap and dazzle of his neighbor.

He would have a ring made, then, fashioned exclusively for Cynthia Coppersmith Kavanagh. He saw their initials somehow entwined inside the band—*ccktak*. But of course he had no earthly idea who to call or where to turn. When someone left a Ross-Simon catalog on the table at the post office, he snatched it up and carried it outside to his car, where he pored over the thing until consciousness returned and he realized he'd sat there with the motor running for a full half hour, steaming in his raincoat like a clam in its shell.

"I'm sorry," he said, looking at her bare ring finger. "If I'd done things right, I would have given you a ring when I proposed."

"I don't really want an engagement ring, dearest. Just a simple gold band would be perfect."

"You're certain?"

"Yes!" she said. "I love simple gold bands."

The image of his mother's wedding band came instantly to mind. It was in his closet, in a box on the shelf, tied by a slender ribbon. He would take it to the store and have it cleaned and engraved and present it at the altar with unspeakable joy and thanksgiving.

He felt he was at last beginning to get things right.

Uncle Billy Watson brushed the leaves and twigs from last night's storm off the seat of a rusting dinette chair and sat down in the backyard of the Porter house, a.k.a. Mitford's town museum.

He gazed dolefully into the sea of towering grass that extended to the rear of the house and then beyond his view. The town crew was supposed to mow the grass once every twelve days; by his count, it was fourteen going on fifteen, and a man could get lost out here and not be heard from again; it was a disgrace the way the town put every kind of diddledaddle ahead of mowing something as proud and fine as their own museum. If he could do it himself, he would, but his arthritis hardly allowed him to get up and down the steps, much less scour a full acre and a quarter with a rusted push mower. He hoped that when he got to Heaven, the Lord would outfit him with a new body and give him a job that *required* something of a man.

But he hadn't come out here to get his dander up. He'd come out to noodle his noggin about a joke to tell at the preacher's wedding, back in that room where they'd all eat cake and ham after the ceremony. Though nobody had said a word about it, the old man knew the preacher would be expecting a joke, he'd be counting on it, and it was his responsibility, his civic duty to tell the best joke he could come up with.

He would never say this to a soul, but it seemed like the preacher getting married so late in life was sort of a joke in itself. It would be a different thing if the father had been married before and had some practice, but as far as anybody knew, he hadn't had any practice.

But who was he to judge other people's setups? Half the town thought he was crazy as a bedbug for living with Rose Watson; even his uncle—who'd come to see them years ago when Rose was still as pretty as a speckled pup—his uncle had said, "They ain't no way I'm understandin' how you put up with this mess."

Her illness seemed to start right after they married, though he'd witnessed, and ignored, warning signs from the day they met. For years, he'd told himself that it was something he'd done wrong, that he hadn't cherished her like the vows said, and maybe God was punishing them both for his ignorance and neglect. Then the doctors found out about the disease he couldn't spell and could barely pronounce, schizophrenia.

On the worst days, he squeezed his eyes shut and remembered the girl he'd seen in the yard of this very house, more than—what was it?—forty-five, maybe fifty years ago. She was barefooted and had her hair tied back with a ribbon. Ragged and dirty from working in the fields since daylight, he'd come up from the valley with a wagonload of tomatoes and roasting ears, carrying a sack of biscuits and fried side meat for his dinner. He'd gone around the village looking for a spot to park his wagon and sell his produce, and saw her standing in her yard. At first he thought she was a statue. Then she moved and the light fell on her in a certain way and he called out, "Would you let a man park his wagon on your road?" And she'd walked out to him and smiled at him and nodded. "Get on down," she said. He'd always remember her first words to him: *Get on down.* He was ashamed that he wasn't wearing shoes, but then he saw that she wasn't, either. She had hung around, looking at him in a way that made him feel uneasy, then happy, and he'd shared his biscuits and side meat with her and she'd gone in the house and brought out a Mason jar of tea so cold and sweet it hurt his teeth. Between times when customers came and went, she talked about herself more than a little. Her beloved brother, Willard, was dead in the war, buried across the ocean in France, and she was looked after by a woman who paid no attention to her. By early afternoon, he'd sold everything but two tomatoes, which he gave to Rose, who said she'd allow him to park his wagon there next week.

They married eighteen months later, against the wishes of his family in the valley, whom he never went back to visit. And there he was, a rough valley boy with no education to speak of, married to a girl with a big inheritance including the finest house in Mitford, and him caning chairs and making birdhouses and doing whatever else he could to hold up his end of the bargain.

But he wouldn't go back and do it any different. Nossir. He'd loved that long-legged girl with the wild eyes more than anything in this world, and could never forget how she used to cling to him and call him Billy Boy and Sweet William, and kiss him with all the innocence of a woods violet.

His chin dropped to his chest and he jerked awake. Here he was sleeping when he had a job to do.

What was the job? For a moment, he couldn't remember. Then it came to him.

His hand trembled as he propped his cane against the tree. "Lord," he said aloud, "I hope You don't mind me askin' You to provide a good joke for th' preacher, don't you know. . . ."

ꝏ

Mayor Esther Cunningham couldn't help herself. Every time she thought about Father Tim getting married, she thought about the way she and Ray had met and courted, and her eyes misted. She did not like her eyes to mist; she had quit crying years ago when her daddy passed. Whenever she felt like crying, she had learned to turn it inside, where it sometimes felt like a Popsicle melting. She had read an article in a magazine at Fancy Skinner's which said that if you turn sorrow in, it will come out—as cancer or something worse, though she couldn't think of anything worse. The article had gone on to say that intimacy with your husband was good for your health, and no matter what else might happen in this life, she and Ray had that in spades; forty-seven years later, they were still holding hands just like on their first date.

Before Ray, Bobby Prestwood had tried everything to get in her good graces, including making a fool of himself in Sunday School when he stood up one morning and told what he was thankful for. "I'm thankful for my Chevy V-8, my mama and daddy, and Esther Lovell!" She didn't give a katy what Bobby Prestwood was thankful for, and told him so at the picnic, which was where she met Ray. He had come late with his cousins, carrying a basket of fried chicken and coleslaw, which he'd made himself. She couldn't believe that anybody that big and tall and good-looking could cook, much less chop cabbage; it just amazed her. She had eyed him up and down to see if he was a sissy, but found no evidence of this. When the cousins invited her to sit with them, she accepted, ate three pieces of Ray's fried chicken with all the trimmings, and took home a wing wrapped in a napkin. Two months later, they were married.

To this day, she'd never met another woman whose husband rubbed her feet, or maybe people just never mentioned it. And not only did Ray rub her feet after she'd worked like a dog all day and half the night in meetings at town hall, he'd have her supper in the oven, which she sometimes took to bed and ate sitting up watching TV, with him lying there patting her leg. "Little darlin'," he might say while he patted.

If she ever had to climb in a bed without Ray Cunningham in it, she would die, she would *go morte,* as Lew Boyd liked to say.

She picked up the phone and dialed home.

"Ray . . ."

She heard Teensy barking in the background. "Hey, sugar babe! It's hot as blazes today, I'll run you up a jar of lemonade in a little bit. What else you need?"

She wouldn't have told him that all she needed was to hear his voice.

Uncle Billy shuffled to the dining room and rifled through stacks of newspaper that the town inspector had threatened to haul off, but had forgotten to do. He was after some copies of *The Farmer's Almanac* that he'd saved for the jokes.

Sweat beaded his forehead and upper lip as he worked through the piles, but not a trace of a *Farmer's Almanac* with its red cover could he find. Dadgummit, he'd hid things in here for years and always managed to find them, and now, not a trace.

He worked his hand around in the pile of *Mitford Muses*, which occupied a space next to the kitchen door, and felt for the familiar shape of an almanac. What was that? He pulled it out and looked. A twenty-dollar bill! He wanted to whoop, but knew better.

If Rose got wind of this twenty, she'd connive every way in creation to yank it out of him. No, by jing, he'd do something he hardly ever did, but often thought about: he'd walk down to the Grill and get an order of fries and bring Rose a surprise milkshake. Besides, he'd gotten two or three of his best jokes at the Grill—maybe that was where he'd find this one.

Careful to put the twenty in the pants pocket without the hole, he abandoned the search for the almanacs and instituted a hurried quest for any other currency he'd once hidden in the vicinity.

Louella Baxter Marshall sat by the window in the sewing room, now her bedroom at Fernbank, looking at the catalog.

The light was good in here and she could clearly see the picture of the dress she'd be wearing to the wedding.

After two days of praying about it and going back and forth from page 42 to page 47, she had showed Miss Sadie her pick. "Green or lavender?" she asked her lifelong friend and sister in Christ.

Miss Sadie didn't hesitate. "Lavender!" she said. "You always looked good in lavender."

Miss Sadie was a little bit like a mama, for it was Miss Sadie who knew Louella's history, who said things like, "When you were a baby, you hated apple butter," or "I remember the time I pulled you to town in the wagon—you hopped out and chased Perry Mackey down the street for a lick on his peppermint stick. You nearly scared him to death!"

Louella didn't remember any of the events Miss Sadie liked to recall, but she'd heard them so often, they'd become as good as real memories. She savored the image of chasing a little white boy down the street to lick his candy, and wondered why on earth she loved apple butter now if she hated it then.

"How you know I *always* look good in this color?"

"When you were about six years old, Mama made you a lavender dress with smocking on the bodice. Don't you remember it, with little pearl buttons? It was such a pretty dress I was half jealous!"

She was disgusted with herself for not remembering. "Don' you think this big white collar too fancy for my face?"

"Posh tosh! Your face may be too fancy for that collar!"

They had both laughed and laughed, then they'd zeroed in on the business of Miss Sadie's final choice. Page 36 was too drab; page 37 was too high in the waist; page 40 was not only shapeless, it had three-quarter-length sleeves, which, as anybody knew, were unflattering all the way back to the pharaohs. Page 41, however, showed promise.

"I like the way it's cut," said Miss Sadie, peering at the dress through a magnifying glass, "but I'm too gray-headed for this color."

"Why, listen at that! Gray-headed is what look *good* wit' blue."

"But it's a pale blue, and it might wash me out."

"No, honey, you might wash *it* out!"

They had laughed again, like children, and decided on the pale blue French crepe with smocked bodice.

Louella held the catalog closer to the window and squinted at the picture.

She wished Moses Marshall could see her all dressed up for the father's wedding. He would look at her and be so proud. Oh, how she'd loved that man from the day she laid eyes on him!

She closed her eyes to rest them and held the picture against her heart, and saw her husband-to-be walking into the kitchen of the Atlanta boardinghouse.

She was fifteen years old, with her hair in cornrows and the sense that something wonderful was about to happen.

Moses Marshall flashed a smile that nearly knocked her winding. She had never seen anybody who looked like this when she was growing up in Mitford. The only people of color in Mitford were old and stooped over.

"Who's th' one baked them good biscuits for supper?" he asked.

She'd been scarcely able to speak. "What you want to know for?"

"'Cause th' one baked them good biscuits, that's th' one I'm goin' to marry."

She had looked at old Miss Sally Lou, who had to stand on tiptoe to peer into a pot on the stove. She was so little and dried up, some said she was a hundred, but

Louella knew she was only eighty-two, and still the boss cook of three meals a day at the boardinghouse.

She had pointed to Miss Sally Lou, afraid to say the plain truth—that she, Louella Baxter, had baked the biscuits herself, three pans full and not one left begging.

Moses Marshall looked his bright, happy look at Miss Sally Lou and walked over and picked her up and swung her around twice before he set her down like a doll. "Fine biscuits, ma'am. Will you jump th' broom wit' me?"

"Git out of my way 'fore I knock you in th' head!" said Miss Sally Lou. "Marry that 'un yonder, she th' one do biscuits, I does yeast rolls."

She was sixteen when they were married at her grandmother's house in Atlanta, where she'd gone to live after leaving Mitford. Her grandmother had cooked the wedding feast, which was topped off with fresh peach cobbler. "Why eat cake when you can eat cobbler?" was what her grandmother always said.

Her years with Moses had been the happiest years of her life, next to those with Miss Sadie. But the Lord had taken Moses home when he was just thirty-nine, and then He'd taken her precious boy in a terrible wreck, leaving her a grandson living in Los Angeles. . . .

She looked out to the green orchard and nodded her head and smiled. "Moses Marshall," she said, "I invite you to sit wit' me at th' weddin,' an' don' be pinchin' and kissin' on me in front of th' good Lord an' ever'body. . . ."

Dooley Barlowe was trying to be happy, but he figured he didn't know what that was supposed to mean. He felt around inside himself, around the area of his heart, maybe, and tried to see if he could make things seem good and right about Father Tim and Cynthia getting married. He'd seen what happened when people lived together under the same roof: They yelled and screamed and fought and said terrible things to each other. He'd seen his daddy go at his mama with a butcher knife more than once, and after his daddy ran off, he'd seen his mama leave for two and three days at a time and depend on him to mind the kids and feed them without any money to buy stuff with.

He remembered stealing a pork loin from the grocery store and getting it home and not knowing how to cook it. He had dropped it in a pot of boiling water with oatmeal and let it cook 'til the water boiled out on the stove, then he carved the meat in five chunks and they tried to eat it and got so sick, he thought they'd all die in the night. Once he'd stolen five cans of creamed corn, so they could all have exactly the same thing and not fight over who got what and how much, and the store manager had caught him and jumped on him really bad, but he'd let him have the corn, saying if he ever did it again he'd be sent to the penitentiary. A woman who overheard the commotion had gone and gotten a can of Harvard beets, a loaf of Wonder bread, a pound of M&Ms, and a quart of buttermilk and gave the items to him in a plastic bag. He remembered that he couldn't stomach buttermilk and the kids wouldn't drink it, either, but they couldn't bear to throw it out and it sat in the refrigerator for maybe a year.

He didn't like to think about these things, he wanted to forget everything that had ever happened before he came here, but sometimes he couldn't. He especially wanted to forget about his little sister, Jessie, because thinking of her being gone and nobody knowing where made him want to cry, and he tried to keep his face as hard and tight and straight as possible so nobody would ever be able to tell what he was thinking.

Sometimes, at night especially, he remembered trying to help his mama when she was drunk, and would suddenly feel a great love for her welling up in him. Then he'd be angry with himself for being stupid, and feel the old and shameful desire for her to die.

Things were just fine for him and Father Tim; he felt safe, finally, like things would be all right. But now he didn't know what would happen. He liked Cynthia, but what if she didn't like him, what if she tried to get him to leave or go back to his mother, if anybody could even find his mother? Or what if Cynthia tried to be his mother? His heart felt cold at such a thought. He wanted his own mother, even if he did hate her and wish he would never see her again as long as he lived.

He was glad that Barnabas came to his room and jumped on the foot of his bed, because it felt good to have a friend. Besides, Barnabas would never tell anyone that he was crying and couldn't stop.

CHAPTER SIX

The Letter

His heart was nearly bursting with a kind of longing, though he had no idea why. After all, he was blessed with everything this life could afford, everything and more.

He sat at his desk in the study and looked out the window into the gloaming as it settled over Baxter Park. Cynthia was working on an illustration that had to go out tomorrow by FedEx, or he would have been at her side, as magnetized to her living presence as his grocery list to the refrigerator.

He drummed his fingers on the desktop.

He didn't want to work on his sermon. He didn't want to take a shower and crawl into bed with a well-loved book from his well-stocked shelves, and he most certainly did not want to turn on the TV and have the clamor pour into this quiet place like some foul Niagara. He was unable to think of anything he wanted to do; there was no seduction in any of the usual pursuits.

Aha. His fingers grew still upon the desktop.

There it was, plain as day:

He wanted to record, somehow, the joy of this breathless thing that had swept him up and overpowered and mesmerized him. Perhaps for most people, people who had been in love again and again, it would not be such a beauteous experience, but it was new to him and dazzling. Yet even in its newness, he felt it slipping away, becoming part of a personal history in which the nuances, the shading, would be lost forever; buried within the consciousness, yes, but paled by time, and then, he feared, vanished altogether.

He opened the desk drawer and took out a writing pad and one of the commercial pens he'd grown to prefer. Though the ink had a noxious odor, he liked the way it flowed onto the page—black, bold, and able.

He knew now what his soul was driving him to. He knew, and he liked the idea immensely.

He would write a poem.

In it, he would tell her everything, he would confess the all of his love, which, by its great and monumental force, had heretofore rendered him dumb as a mackerel.

With her, he experienced a galaxy . . . no, an entire universe of feelings, yet they continually displayed themselves as the western portion of the state of Rhode Island: *Youarebeautifultome Ishallloveyoueternallywillyoumarrymeandmakemethehappiestmanwhoeverdrewbreath,* period, end of declaration.

He was amazed at how far he'd gotten with this extraordinary woman by the utterance of the most rudimentary expressions of love, all of them sincere beyond measure, and yet, they were words too simple and words too few; not once had they been equal to the character, the beauty, or the spirit of the one to whom they were addressed.

He knew, now, why people wanted to shout from rooftops, yet he couldn't imagine it to have great effect, in the end. One would clamber onto the roof and, teetering on some gable or chimney pot, bellow until one was hoarse as a bullfrog, "I love! I love!"

And what would people on the street do? They would look up, they would shrug, they would roll their eyes, they would say:

So?

He bounded happily from the chair and went to the kitchen to put the kettle on. Clearly, shouting from the rooftops had been a fleeting thing in the history of the lovestruck, not long enjoyed as a certified expression of ardor. Indeed, what had done the trick each and every time? Poetry! And history had proved it!

"'I love thee,'" he recited as he filled the kettle, "'. . . to the level of every day's Most quiet need, by sun and candlelight . . . I love thee freely, as men strive for Right . . .'"

There! That was getting down to it. The only problem was that E. B. Browning had already written it.

He stood musing by the stove in a kind of fog that made him forget momentarily where he was and what he was up to, until the kettle whistled and he awoke and found himself oddly joyful to be dropping the bags into the teapot and pouring the steaming water therein.

He clamped the lid on the pot and, leaving it to the business of steeping, returned to the study and visited his bookshelves. He couldn't readily put his hand on a volume of love poetry, but surely he'd find something here to spark a thought, to get his blood up.

He chose a small blue volume that he'd used a time or two in marital counseling, and opened it at random.

"'I feel sad when I don't see you,'" he read aloud from a letter by a nineteenth-century American suitor. "'Be married, why won't you? And come to live with me. I will make you as happy as I can. You shall not be obliged to work hard, and when you are tired, you may lie in my lap and I will sing you to rest . . .'"

There's a good fellow! he thought.

"'. . . because I love you so well, I will not make you bring in wood and water, or feed the pig, or milk the cow, or go to the neighbors to borrow milk. Will you be married?'"

He shoved the book upon the shelf, took down another, and thumbed through the section on all things marital.

"'I love you no longer; on the contrary, I detest you . . .'" Napoleon Bonaparte to Josephine, wrong section.

Ah, well, here was one for the books, something Evelyn Waugh had trotted out in a letter of proposal. "'I can't advise you in my favour because I think it would be beastly for you, but think how nice it would be for me!'"

Would it be beastly for Cynthia? Living with him, an old stick in the mud? He shook the thought away and licked his right forefinger and turned to another page.

"'You have set a crown of roses on my youth and fortified me against the disaster of our days. Your courageous gaiety has inspired me with joy. Your tender faithfulness has been a rock of security and comfort. I have felt for you all kinds of love at once. I have asked much of you and you have never failed me. You have intensified all colours, heightened all beauty, deepened all delight. . . .'" Duff Cooper, writing to his future wife in the war-dark year of 1918, had known how to get down to brass tacks, all right. Maybe he could do something with the idea of courageous gaiety; he had always thought Cynthia courageous.

He sighed deeply. In truth, this was going nowhere. It was a waste of precious time to try and glean from another man's brain. There'd be no more lollygagging.

He dashed again to the kitchen and poured a mug of tea, then added a little milk and stirred it well, and returned to his desk and sat, gazing at the mug, the pad, and the pen, and the nightfall dark against his window.

He considered that he had written hymns to God, several in his time, but he'd never done anything like this, never! He knew that God was familiar with his very innards and that He perceived the passion of his heart full well; thus he had not sweated greatly over lines that were awkward here or a tad sophomoric there, but this . . .

"*Write!*" he bellowed aloud.

Barnabas bolted from the rug by the sofa and trotted to his master and stood by the desk. The rector turned his head slowly, and for a moment each looked soulfully into the other's eyes.

Dearest love . . . , he wrote at last, *tender one . . . my heart's joy . . .*

He drew a line through the feeble words and began again:

Loveliest angel of light and life . . .

What about something from the Song of Solomon? On second thought, scratch that. The Song still made him blush. Whoever drummed up the notion that it was about Christ and the church . . .

He nibbled his right forefinger and mused upon lines from Shakespeare; he chewed his lower lip and called to mind Keats; he sank his head onto his arms on the desktop and contemplated Robert Browning's fervent avowal, "All my soul follows you, love . . . and I live in being yours."

Blast and double blast. The good stuff had already been written.

He talked to himself with some animation as he trotted up Main Street from Lord's Chapel. What if Shakespeare had never put pen to paper because the good stuff had already been written? In truth, what if he refused one morning to preach because all the good sermons had already been preached?

Ha!

On the other side of the Irish Shop's display window, Minnie Lomax examined the bent head and hunched shoulders of the village priest as he blew past, his mouth moving in what she supposed was prayer.

He didn't look at all like a man besotted with love, not in her view.

Why was he staring at the sidewalk when he might be looking into the heavens, or whistling, or waving to her through the window as he usually did? He was scared of what he'd let himself in for, that's what! Sixty-something and getting married for the *first time*? The very thought gave her the shivers.

She had never married, and never wanted to. Well, not never, exactly. She had wanted to once, and look what happened. She sniffed and smoothed her cardigan over her thin hips and took a Kleenex from her pocket and blew her nose, then turned around to the empty store, wondering what she might do to lure traffic through the door today. Boiled wool had a terrible go of it during the summer; next year she would advise the owner to put in more cotton and linen, for heaven's sake, and get shed of the entire lot of those hideous crocheted caps.

He would choose each word as carefully as his mother had chosen peaches off Lot Stringman's truck. "Let me pick them out for you, Miz Kavanagh." "No, thank you, Mr. Stringman," she would say, "I like the doing of it myself."

Finally despairing that writing a poem was beyond his endowment, he had decided to be content with writing a letter.

Peach by perfect peach, that is how he would choose his words. . . .

Sunday afternoon, four o'clock, a breeze stirring through the open windows

My Own,

Consider how these two small words have the power to move and shake me, and take my breath away! I am raised to a height I have never before known, somewhere above the clouds that hide the mountain-rimmed valleys and present a view of floating peaks. I have been comfortable for years, haplessly rooted in myself like a turnip, and now am not comfortable at all, but stripped of everything that is easeful and familiar, and filled with everything that is tremulous and alive; I am a spring lamb upon new legs. Every nerve is exposed to you, my dearest love, and my thankfulness for this gift from God knows no bounds, no bounds! Indeed, He has saved the best for last, and that He should have saved it at all, set it aside for me, is a miracle. A miracle! Let no one ever say or even think that God does not work miracles, still; every common day, every common life is filled with them, as you know better than anyone I have ever met. You, who see His light and life in the dullest blade of grass, have taught my own eye to look for and find His magnitude abounding everywhere.

Though you are merely steps away, beyond the hedge, I long for you as if you were in Persia, and yet, your presence is with me, your very fragrance clings to the shirt I wear.

I have given my heart completely only once, and that was to Him. Now He has, Himself, set aside in my heart a room for you. It is large and open and suffused with light, with no walls or boundaries to stifle us, and He has graciously fashioned it to give us warmth and shelter and joyous freedom until the end of our days.

May this be only the first of many times I thank you for all you are to me, and for the precious and inimitable gift of your love.

Please know that I shall set a watch upon myself—to make every effort to bring you the happiness you so richly deserve, and, by His grace, to place your needs before my own.

May God bless you with His greatest tenderness now and always, my sweetheart, my soon-to-be wife.

Timothy

He sat as if drained; there was nothing left of him, nothing at all, he was parchment through which light might be seen.

"Barnabas," he murmured.

His good dog stirred at his feet.

"I have a mission for you, old friend." He folded the letter, regretting that he'd written it on paper from a mere notepad. Ah, well, what was done was done. He placed the letter in an envelope and thought carefully how he might address it.

In a letter hidden inside an envelope, one might say whatever one wished, but the outside of the envelope was quite another thing, being completely exposed, as it were, to . . . to what? The hedge? The sky?

My love, my blessing, my neighbor, he scrawled with some abandon.

He licked the flap and pressed it down and sat for a moment with it under his hand, then took it to the kitchen and found a length of twine, which he looped around the neck of his patient dog. Lacking a hole punch, he stuck the tip of a steak knife through the corner of the envelope and ran the twine through the hole and tied it in a knot.

"There!" he said aloud.

He walked with Barnabas down the back

steps and across the yard to the hedge. "OK, boy, take it to Cynthia!"

Barnabas lifted his leg against a rhododendron.

"Take it to Cynthia!" he said, wagging his finger in the direction of the little yellow house. "Over there! Go see Cynthia!"

Barnabas turned and looked at him with grave indifference.

"Cat!" he hissed. *"Cynthia's house! Cat, cat, cat!"* That ought to do it.

Barnabas sniffed a few twigs that lay in the grass, then sat down and scratched vigorously.

Rats, what a dumb idea. In the old days, a fellow would have sent his valet or his coachman or some such, and here he was trying to send a dog—he deserved what he was getting.

"Go, dadgummit! Go to Cynthia's back door, that's where you love to go when you're not supposed to!"

Barnabas gazed at him for a moment, then turned and bounded through the hedge and across her yard and up the steps to her stoop, where he sat and pressed his nose against the screen door, peering in.

He suddenly felt ten years old. Why couldn't he think straight for five minutes in a row? His dog might sit at that door 'til kingdom come, with Cynthia having no clue Barnabas was out there. Should he run to the door and knock to alert her, then run away again?

This was suddenly the most ridiculous mess he'd gotten himself into in . . . ever. His face flamed.

"Timothy?" It was Cynthia, calling to him through her studio window. He'd utterly forgotten about her studio window.

"Umm, yes?"

"Why are you hiding behind the hedge?"

He was mortified. *I have no idea,* he wanted to say. "There's a *delivery*"—he fairly thundered the word—"at your back door."

"Oh," she said.

He waited, covering his face with his hands.

"My goodness!" he heard her exclaim as she opened the screen door. "A letter on a string!"

Surely he would regret this.

" 'My love, my blessing, my neighbor'!" she crowed.

Did she have to inform the whole neighborhood?

"Go tell your master that I've received his most welcome missive . . . which I can barely get off the string. Ugh! . . . Oh, rats, wait 'til I get the scissors."

His dog waited.

"And further," she said, coming back and snipping the letter off, "do tell him I shall endeavor to respond promptly. However, my dear Barnabas, do not harbor, even for a moment, the *exceedingly* foolish hope that it will be delivered by Violet."

The screen door slapped behind her.

The deed done, his dog arose, shook himself, and came regally down the steps, across the yard, and through the hedge, where, wearing the remains of the twine around his neck, he sat and gazed at his master with a decided air of disdain, if not utter disgust.

CHAPTER SEVEN

The Prayer

She pressed the letter to her heart, wishing the power of its message to enter her very soul and cause her to believe with the writer what an extraordinary benediction had come to them.

Yes, she loved him; in truth, more than life itself. And yet, the fear was beginning to creep in, the fear she had at last grown wise enough to recognize—that she could not please him and give him the joy that he above all others, deserved; the fear that Timothy, like Elliott, would not find her valuable enough for any true purpose; the fear that her priest, her neighbor, and now her betrothed, might discover in her some "terrible lack," as Elliott had called her inability to bear children.

Only weeks earlier, she had wept in despair that Timothy Kavanagh would ever be able to abandon his own raw fear and surrender his heart.

Now she bowed her head and wept because, at last, he had.

She stood at the kitchen sink, spooning an odorous lump of congealed cat food into Violet's dish.

Drawing her breath sharply, she stared at the cat bowl that she had just filled without knowing it.

She felt stricken. What had she done when she accepted his proposal with such unbearable eagerness and joy? Had she rashly agreed to something in which she might prove a bitter disappointment to both Timothy and herself?

And another thing—could she, who had often felt thrown away, be a friend and guide to a thrown-away boy? She thought she could, she knew she wanted to—for Dooley's sake and her own.

She put the bowl on the floor and walked down the hall to her studio and stood at the window, gazing across the hedge to the rectory. There was his stone chimney, his slate roof, his bedroom window beneath the gable. . . .

How often she had found solace in merely looking upon his house, the place where he would be working in his study, snoring by his fire, brushing his dog, commandeering his wayward boy, living his life.

She'd begun by having the most terrific crush on him, like a pathetic schoolgirl; it had been the sort of thing that made her blush at the sight of him, and caused her skin to tingle when she heard his voice. Worse, there had been long lapses in concentration that afflicted her for months on end.

She had plotted ways to meet him on the street, and once thumped onto the bench in front of the Main Street Grill, affecting a turned ankle that delayed her jaunt to The Local. He had, indeed, come by, just as she'd hoped, and sat with her and smiled at her in a way that made her nearly speechless until, finally, she fled the bench, forgetting to limp, and avoided him altogether for several weeks.

She remembered, too, the day she had prayed and marched boldly to his back door. Her heart thundered under her jumper as she asked to borrow a cup of sugar to make a cake. Having no intention of making a cake, she worried whether, in some priestly way, he might see through such guile and find her out. But he had invited her in and fed her from the remains of his own supper and she had seen something in his eyes, some kindness that had nearly broken her heart with its plainness and simplicity. And then his dog, attached to the handle of the silver drawer by a leash, had yanked the drawer out, sending forks, knives, and spoons clattering about the kitchen and skidding into the hallway. They had dropped to their knees as one, hooting with laughter as they collected the errant flatware. Even then, she knew that something had been sealed between them, and that it was laughter that had sealed it

It had been years since Elliott walked out—the divorce papers arrived by certified mail the following day—and in those years, not one soul had made her mouth go dry as cotton and her knees turn to water. Oh, how she had despised the torment of loving like a girl instead of like . . . like a sophisticated woman, whatever that might be.

That early, awkward time had also been irresistibly sweet. But now this—confusion and distress and alarm, and yes, the oddly scary thoughts of the women of Lord's Chapel who for years had stood around him like a hedge of thorns, protecting him as their very own; keeping him, they liked to believe, from foolish stumbles; feeding him meringues and layer cake at every turn; mothering and sistering him as if this were their life's calling. She saw, now, something she'd only glimpsed before, and that was the way an unmarried priest is thought to belong to the matrons of the church, lock, stock, and barrel.

More than once she'd waited at his side, feeling gauche and adolescent, as they clucked over him—inquiring after his blood sugar, flicking an imaginary hair from his lapel, ordering him to take a week off, and coyly insisting he never stray beyond the town limits. They were perfectly harmless, every one, and she despised herself for such cheap and petty thoughts, but they were real thoughts, and now that the word was out, she felt his flock sizing her up in a fresh, even severe way.

Yet, for all their maternal indulgence of their priest, she knew they underestimated him most awfully. She had heard a member of the Altar Guide wondering how anyone "so youthful and sure of herself" could be attracted to their "dear old priest who is going bald as a hen egg and diabetic to boot."

Indeed, he wasn't merely the mild and agreeable man they perceived him to be; he was instead a man of the richest reserves of strength and poise, of the deepest tenderness and most enormous wit and gallantry.

From the beginning, she found him to possess an ardor for his calling that spoke to her heart and mind and soul in such a deep and familiar way, she felt as if he were long-lost kin, returned at last from a distant shore. He had felt this, too, this connection of some vital force in himself with her own vitality, and he had been knocked back, literally, as if by the thunder-striking power of a summer storm.

She had known she would never again be given such a connection, and she had moved bravely toward it, toward its heat, toward its center, while he had drawn back, shaken.

" 'Love bade me welcome,' " he had once quoted from George Herbert, " 'but my soul drew back.' " She found a delicate irony in the fact that George Herbert had been a clergyman.

She looked at the handwritten sheet

pinned above her drawing board, something she had copied at the Mitford library from an old book by Elizabeth Goudge:

> She had long accepted the fact that happiness is like swallows in spring. It may come and nest under your eaves or it may not. You cannot command it. When you expect to be happy you are not, when you don't expect to be happy there is suddenly Easter in your soul, though it be midwinter. Something, you do not know what, has broken the seal upon that door in the depth of your being that opens upon eternity.

Eternity!

She moved from the window and walked quickly to the kitchen. She would do something that, if only for the briefest hour, had the power to solve everything, to offer certain and absolute consolation.

She would cook.

She removed the chicken from the refrigerator, already rubbed with olive oil and crushed garlic, with half a lemon tucked into its cavity. She misted olive oil into her ancient iron skillet, placed the bird on its back, and ground pepper and sea salt onto its plump flesh. From a glass of water on the windowsill she removed a pungent stalk of fresh rosemary and stuck it under the breast skin. The top of the green stalk waved forth like a feather from a hat band.

She turned the stove dial to 450, where it would remain for thirty minutes before being set at 350 for an hour, and slid the raw feast onto the middle rack.

The wrenching thing, she knew in her heart, was having no one to talk with about it all, and whose fault was that but her own? Had she not worked like a common stevedore since coming to Mitford, making a way for her work instead of making friends? Oh, yes, she was liked well enough, she really was, but there was no trusted friend to whom she might pour her heart out. There was no one, not a soul.

Except . . . she smiled at the thought . . . the priest himself. Her heart warmed suddenly, and lifted up. Hadn't she confessed something to him only yesterday?

"They don't like me," she had said, despising the whine she heard in her voice. "They did, of course, until they learned you were actually going to marry me, but now . . ."

"Nonsense!" he'd said with feeling. "They think the *world* of you!"

That was apparently the most profound compliment a Southerner could pay, to insist that one was thought the "world" of!

She realized she wouldn't finish the illustration as she'd promised her editor; she would finish it tomorrow, instead. She, who was ever loath to break a promise, would break this one.

"Timothy?" she said when he answered the phone. "Can you come over?" Her heart was pounding, and there was a distinct quaver in her voice; she was warbling like a canary.

"I'm scared, dearest, scared to death."

She loved the way he sat with her, not saying anything in particular, not probing, not pushing her, just sitting on her love seat. Perhaps what she liked best was that he always looked comfortable wherever he was, appearing glad to live within his skin and not always jumping out of it like some men, like James, her editor, who was everlastingly clever and eloquent and ablaze with wild ideas that succeeded greatly for him, while with Timothy the thing that succeeded was quietude, something rich and deep and . . . nourishing, a kind of spiritual chicken soup simmering in some far reach of the soul.

"Tell me," he said at last. "Tell me everything. I'm your priest, after all." She thought his smile dazzling, a dazzling thing to come out of quietude. She had pulled a footstool to the love seat and sat close to him.

"I'm terribly afraid I can't make you happy," she said.

"But that was my fear! I finally kicked it out the back door and now it's run over here."

"It's not funny, Timothy."

"I'm not laughing."

He took her hands in his and lightly kissed the tips of her fingers and she caught the scent of him, the innocence of him, and her spirit mounted up again.

"Why don't we pray together?" he said. "Just let our hearts speak to His. . . ."

Sitting at his feet, she bowed her head and closed her eyes and he stroked her shoulder. Though the clock ticked in the hallway, she supposed that time was standing still, and that she might sit with him in this holy reverie, forever.

"Lord," he said, simply, "here we are."

"Yes, Lord, here we are."

They drew in their breath as one, and let it out in a long sigh, and she realized for a moment how the very act of breathing in His presence was balm.

"Dear God," he said, "deliver Your cherished one from feeling helpless to receive the love You give so freely, so kindly, from the depths of Your being. Help us to be as large as the love You've given us, sometimes it's too great for us, Lord, even painful in its power. Tear away the old fears, the old boundaries that no longer contain anything of worth or importance, and by Your grace, make Cynthia able to seize this bold, fresh freedom. . . ."

"Yes, Lord," she prayed, "the freedom I've never really known before, but which You've faithfully shown me in glimmers, in epiphanies, in wisps as fragile as . . . light from Your new moon!"

He pressed her hand, feeling in it the beating of her pulse.

"Father, deliver me from the fear to love wholly and completely, I who chided this good man for his own fears, his own weakness, while posing, without knowing it a pose, as confident and bold. You've seen through that, Lord, You've . . . You've found me out for what I am . . ."

There was a long silence, filled by the ticking of the clock.

". . . a frightened seven-year-old who stands at the doorlooking for a father and mother who . . . do not come home.

"Even after years of knowing You as a Father who is always home, I sometimes feel—I feel a prisoner of old and wrenching fears, and I'm ashamed of my fear, and the darkness that prevents me from stepping into the light. . . ."

"You tell us in Your Word," he prayed, "that You do not give us the spirit of fear—"

"But of power and of love and a sound mind!" she whispered, completing the verse from the second letter to Timothy.

"And so, Lord, I rebuke the Enemy who would employ every strategy to deny Your children the blessing of Your grace."

"Yes, Lord!"

"Help us to receive Your peace and courage, Your confidence and power," he said.

"Yes, Lord!"

"Thank you for being with us now, and in the coming weeks and coming years."

"And Father," she said, "please give me

the grace to love Dooley as You love him, and the patience to encourage and support and understand him, for I wish with all my heart that we might grow together in harmony, as a true family." She took a deep and satisfying breath. "And now, Lord . . ."

As the prayer neared its end, they spoke in unison as they had recently begun to do in their evening prayers.

". . . create in us a clean heart . . . renew a right spirit within us . . . and fill us with Your Holy Spirit . . . through Christ our Lord . . . amen."

He helped her from the footstool and she sat beside him on the love seat and breathed the peace that settled over them like a shawl.

"There will be many times when fear breaks in," he said, holding her close. "We can never be taken prisoner if we greet it with prayer."

"Yes!" she whispered, feeling a weight rolled away like the stone from the sepulcher.

"I smelled the chicken as I came through the hedge."

"Dinner in twenty minutes?" she murmured.

"I thought you'd never ask," he said.

CHAPTER EIGHT

The Preamble

On the morning of September seventh, in the upstairs guest room of the rectory, Bishop Stuart Cullen checked his vestments for any signs of wrinkles or unwanted creases, found none, then took his miter from the box and set it on the bureau, mindful that his crozier was in the trunk of the car, as were his black, polished shoes and an umbrella in case of rain.

Rummaging about the room in a pair of magenta boxer shorts given him by his suffragan, he hummed snatches of a Johnny Cash tune as Martha Cullen sat up in bed and read an issue of *Country Life* magazine that Puny had placed on the night table three years ago and faithfully dusted ever since. Studying a feature on knot gardens, she was utterly unmindful of the bishop's rendition of "Ring of Fire" as he enjoyed a long, steaming shower that caused water in the shower across the hall to trickle upon the rector's head in a feeble stream.

Under the miserly drizzle, the rector counted his blessings that the bishop would be preaching this morning and he celebrating, a veritable holiday in the Caymans, as far as he was concerned. In truth, he feared that if he opened his mouth to deliver wisdom of any sort, it would pour forth as some uncertified language, resulting not from the baptism of the Holy Spirit but of something akin to panic, or worse. He despaired that the custard had vanished in the night, and fear and trembling had jumped into its place with both feet.

In his room across the hall, Dooley sat on the side of his bed and felt the creeping, lopsided nausea that came with the aroma of baking ham as it rose from the kitchen. He said three four-letter words in a row, and was disappointed when his stomach still felt sick.

He hoped his voice wouldn't crack during the hymn. Though he'd agreed to sing a cappella, he didn't trust a cappella. If you hit a wrong note, there was nothing to cover you. He wished there were trumpets or something really loud behind him, but no,

Cynthia wanted "Dooley's pure voice." Gag.

"God," he said aloud, "don't let me sound weird. Amen." He had no idea that God would really hear him or prevent him from sounding weird, but he thought it was a good idea to ask.

He guessed he was feeling better about stuff. Yesterday, Father Tim spent the whole day taking him places, plus they'd run two miles with Barnabas and gone to Sweet Stuff after. Then, Cynthia had given him a hug that nearly squeezed his guts out. "Dooley," she said, "I really care about you."

When he heard that, he felt his face getting hard. He didn't want it to, but it was trained that way. He could tell she really meant it, but she'd have to prove she meant it before he would smile at her; he knew she wanted him to smile. Maybe he would someday, but not now. Now he was trying to keep from puking up his gizzard because he had to sing a song he didn't even like, at a wedding he still wasn't sure of.

In the kitchen of the little yellow house beyond the hedge, Cynthia Coppersmith stood barefoot in her aging chenile robe, her hair in pink foam curlers, eating half a hotdog from the refrigerator and drinking coffee so strong it possessed the consistency of tapioca.

On arriving home last night from the country club dinner party where, out of courtesy, she'd picked at a salad, she had boiled a hotdog and eaten the first half of it in a bun with what she thought was mustard but was, in fact, horseradish, loosely the age of her expiring Boston fern. It was the first true nourishment she'd recently been able to take, except for a rock shrimp and three cherry tomatoes at Friday's bridal luncheon. She ate the remains of the hotdog in two bites and, feeling her lagging appetite suddenly stimulated, foraged in the refrigerator until she found a piece of Wednesday's broiled flounder, which she spritzed with the juice of a geriatric lemon and, standing at the sink, consumed with gusto.

Two blocks south, Esther Bolick peered out her kitchen window as a straggle of rain clouds parted to reveal the sun. "Happy is th' bride th' sun shines on!" she announced with relief.

Going briskly to the oven, she removed three pans of scratch cake layers to a cooling rack, and stood with her hands on her hips in a baby doll nightgown and bedroom shoes with the faces of bunnies. She gazed with satisfaction at the trio of perfect yellow moons, then trotted across the kitchen for another cup of decaf, the black pupils of the bunnies' plastic eyes rolling and clicking like dice.

She would go to Sunday School and the eleven o'clock, then come home and ice the cake and let it sit 'til she carried it to church at four. She and Gene would do what they usually did when hauling around a three-layer—put newspaper on the floor of the cargo area, and while Gene drove, she would sit back there on a stool and hold the cake to keep it from sliding around in its cardboard box. Without a van, there was no way on God's green earth to follow her calling unless you were making sheet cakes, which she utterly despised and would not be caught dead doing. The icing would go on at home, but she'd put the pearls and lilies on at church in one of the Sunday School rooms. Then she'd take the shelves out of the church fridge and pop the whole thing in 'til just before the thundering horde hit the reception.

She removed the hair net from her head and stuck it in the knife drawer.

Four blocks north, Uncle Billy Watson took the wire hanger from the nail on the wall and squinted at the black wool suit, inherited from his long-dead brother-in-law. Its heaviness had bowed down the arms of the coat hanger, giving the whole thing a dejected appearance.

"Dadgummit," he said under his breath. There was a spot on the right lapel as big as a silver dollar; it looked like paint—or was it vanilla pudding? In his pajamas, he shuffled to the kitchen, where he could see in a better light.

Miss Rose was sitting in her chair by the refrigerator, peeling potatoes with a knife too dull to cut butter. "What are you doing, Bill Watson?"

"Cleanin' my coat."

"You'll not be getting *my* goat!" she said, indignant.

His wife was going deaf as a doorknob, and there wasn't a thing he could do about it. She wouldn't even discuss hearing aids, let alone ask the county to buy her a pair.

"What are you wearin' to the weddin'?" he shouted.

"What wedding?"

"Th' preacher's weddin' this evenin' at five o'clock!"

"Five o'clock!" she squawked. "That's suppertime!"

"Well, I cain't help if it is, hit's th' preacher's weddin' an' we're a-goin'." Hadn't he talked about this wedding 'til he was blue in the face, even picked out three dresses she had bitterly rejected? And now this.

He wagged his head and sighed. "Lord have *mercy*."

"What about Percy?" she demanded.

The old man scrubbed at the lapel with a wet dishrag. Some days he could put on a smiley face and go about his business just fine, some days Rose Watson tested his faith, yes, she did. He'd have to trot to church this morning and sit there asking forgiveness for what he was thinking. He'd also be thanking the Lord for the joke. Don't tell him that God Almighty didn't answer foolish prayers!

Four blocks northwest, Hessie Mayhew lay snoring in her double bed with the faded flannel sheets and vintage Sears mattress. She had taken two Benadryl caps last night to dry up her sinuses after a day of messing with lady's-mantel and hydrangeas. Hydrangeas always did something to her sinuses, they had drained like a tap as she plowed through people's yards, taking what she wanted without asking. She'd even ducked behind the Methodist chapel, where a thick hedge of hydrangeas flowered magnificently every year, and took her pick of the huge blooms.

People knew who she was, they knew whose wedding this was; if she'd stopped to ask permission, they'd have said help yourself, take all you want! So why stop and ask, that was her philosophy! People should be proud for her to rogue their flowers, seeing they made so many people happy. *I declare,* she once imagined someone saying, *Hessie Mayhew stripped every peony bush in my yard today, and I'm just* tickled *about it!*

For her money, the hydrangeas were a week shy of the best color, but did people who set wedding dates ever stop and think of such things? Of course not, they just went blindly on. If she lived to marry again, which she sometimes hoped she would, she'd do it in May, when lily of the valley was at it peak.

On her screened porch, a decrepit porcelain bathtub boasted a veritable sea of virgin's bower and hydrangeas.

In her double kitchen sink, Blue Mist spirea, autumn anemone, Queen Anne's lace, artemisia, and knotweed drank thirstily. Inside the back door, buckets of purple coneflowers, autumn clematis, cosmos, and wild aster sat waiting. On the counter above the dishwasher, a soup pot of pink Duet and white Garden Party roses mingled with foxtail grass, Jerusalem artichoke, dog hobble, and panicles of the richly colored pokeberry. A small butterfly that had ridden in, drugged, on a coneflower, came to itself and visited the artemisia.

At seven-thirty, Hessie Mayhew turned on her side, moaning a little due to the pain in her lower back, and though a team of helpers was due to arrive at eight, she slept on.

In her home a half mile from town, Puny Guthrie crumbled two dozen strips of crisp, center-cut bacon into the potato salad and gave it one last, heaving stir. Everybody would be plenty hungry by six or six-thirty, and she'd made enough to feed a corn shuckin', as her granpaw used to say. She had decided to leave out the onions, since it was a wedding reception and very dressy. She'd never thought dressing up and eating onions were compatible; onions were for picnics and eating at home in the privacy of your own family.

Because Cynthia and the father didn't

want people to turn out for the reception and go home hungry, finger foods were banned. They wanted to give everybody a decent supper, even if they would have to eat it sitting on folding chairs from Sunday School. What with the father's ham, Miss Louella's yeast rolls, Miss Olivia's raw vegetables and dip, her potato salad, and Esther Bolick's three-layer orange marmalade, she didn't think they'd have any complaints. Plus, there would be ten gallons of tea, not to mention decaf, and sherry if anybody wanted any, but she couldn't imagine why anybody would. She'd once taken a sip from the father's decanter, and thought it tasted exactly like aluminum foil, though she'd never personally tasted aluminum foil except when it got stuck to a baked potato.

She thought of her own wedding and how she had walked down the aisle on Father Tim's arm. She had felt like a queen, like she was ten feet tall, looking at everything and everybody with completely new eyes. Halfway down the aisle, she nearly burst into tears, then suddenly she soared above tears to something higher, something that took her breath away, and she knew she would never experience anything like it again. Later, when she called Father Tim

"Father," she was struck to find she said it as if he really were her father, it wasn't just some religious name that went with a collar. Ever since that moment, she'd felt she was his daughter, in a way that no one except herself could understand. And hadn't he been the one to pray that parade prayer that brought Joe Joe to the back door and into her life forever? She had been cleaning the downstairs rectory toilet when Joe Joe came to the back, because she hadn't heard him knocking at the front. When she saw him, her heart did a somersault, because he was the cutest, most handsome person she'd ever seen outside of a TV show or magazine.

"Father Tim said he might have a candy wrapper in the pocket of his brown pants, if you could send it, please."

She knew immediately that this policeman had been raised right, saying "please." Not too many people said please anymore, much less thank you, she thought it was a shame.

She had invited him in and given him a glass of tea and he perched on the stool where Father Tim sat and read his mail, and she went upstairs and looked in the father's brown pants pockets and there it was, wadded up. Why anybody would want to carry around a wadded-up candy wrapper . . .

" 'Scuse my apron," she remembered saying. She would never forget the look in his eyes.

"You look really good in an apron," he said, turning beet red.

She'd never been told such a thing and had no idea what to say. She handed him the candy wrapper and he put it in a little Ziploc bag without taking his eyes off her.

She thought she was going to melt and run down in a puddle. Then he bolted off the stool and was out the door and gone and that was that. Until he came back the very next day when she was cooking lima beans.

"Hey," she said through the screen door as he bounded up the steps. By now, she knew that the whole police force was working on the big jewel theft at Lord's Chapel.

"You're under arrest," he said, blushing again.

For a moment, she was terrified that this might be true, then she saw the big grin on his face.

"What're th' charges?"

"Umm, well . . ." He dropped his head and gazed at his shoes.

She thought it must be awful to be a grown man who blushed like a girl.

He jerked his head up and looked her in the eye. “You’re over the legal limit of bein’ pretty.”

She giggled. “What’re you goin’ to do about it?” Boy howdy, that had flown right out of her mouth without even thinking.

“Umm, goin’ to ask you to a movie in Wesley, how’s that?”

“Is it R? I don’t see R.”

“I don’t know,” he said, appearing bewildered.

“You could look in the newspaper, or call,” she said. She could scarcely get her breath. She had never noticed before that a police uniform looked especially good, it was like he was home on leave from the armed forces.

“Will you see, umm, PG-13?”

“Depending.” Why on earth was she being so hard to get along with? Her mouth was acting like it had a mind of its own.

“My grandmother’s th’ *mayor*!” he exclaimed.

“That’s nice,” she said. This was going nowhere. She felt she was fluttering around in space and couldn’t get her toes on the ground. Suddenly realizing again that she was wearing her apron, she snatched it up and over her head and stood there, feeling dumb as a rock.

"So, just trust me," he said. "We'll find a good movie if we have to go all th'way to . . ." He hesitated, thinking. *"Johnson City!"*

"Thank you," she said, "I'd enjoy goin' to th' movies with you."

After he left, she felt so addled and weak in the knees that she wanted to lie down, but would never do such a thing in the father's house; she didn't even *sit* down on the job, except once in a while to peel peaches or snap string beans.

She walked around the kitchen several times, trying to hold something in, she didn't know what it was. She ended up at the back door, where it suddenly came busting out.

It was a shout.

She put the plastic cover on the potato salad bowl and smiled, remembering that she'd stood at the screen door for a long time, with tears of happiness running down her cheeks.

Having had their flight canceled on Saturday due to weather, Walter and Katherine Kavanagh arrived at the Charlotte airport at 11:35 a.m. Sunday morning, following a mechanical delay of an hour and a half at La Guardia. They stood at the baggage carousel, anxiously seeking her black bag, which contained not only her blue faille suite for the wedding, but the gift they'd taken great pains to schlep instead of ship.

"Gone to Charlottesville, Virginia!" said the baggage claim authority, peering into his monitor. "How about that?"

From her greater height of six feet, Katherine surveyed him with a look capable of icing the wings of a 747.

"Sometimes they go to Charleston!" he announced, refusing to wither under her scorn. He was used to scorn; working in an airline baggage claim department was all about scorn.

Miss Sadie Baxter sat at her dressing table in her slip and robe, near the open window of the bedroom she'd occupied since she was nine years old. The rain clouds had rolled away, the sun was shining, and the birds were singing—what more could any human want or ask for?

She carefully combed the gray hair from her brush, rolled it into a tidy ball, and let it fall soundlessly into the wastebasket that bore the faded decal of a camellia blossom.

Where had the years gone? One day she'd sat here brushing hair the color of chestnuts, and the next time she looked up, she was old and gray. She remembered sitting on this same stool, looking into this same mirror, reading Willard Porter's love letter and believing herself to be beautiful. . . .

"Willard!" she whispered, recalling the letter she had committed to memory, the letter he wrote on her twenty-first birthday:

You may know that I am building a house in the village, on the green where Amos Medford grazed his cows. Each stone that was laid in the foundation was laid with the hope that I might yet express the loving regard I have for you, Sadie.

I am going to give this house a name, trusting that things may eventually be different between us. I will have it engraved on a cedar beam at the highest point in the attic, with the intention that its message may one day give you some joy or pleasure.

Perhaps, God willing, your father will soon see that I have something to offer, and relent. Until then, dear Sadie, I can offer only my fervent love and heartfelt devotion.

Soon afterward, Willard had been killed and buried in France, and many years went by before she learned the name he had engraved on the beam.

" 'For lo, the winter is past . . . ,' " she murmured, gazing from her window into the orchard. Learning the name, Winterpast, had indeed given her much joy and pleasure.

" '. . . the rain is over and gone. The flowers appear on the earth; the time of the singing of birds is come. . . .' "

The time of the singing of birds had come for the father and Cynthia.

Miss Sadie looked into the mirror and smiled. Yes, it was their time, now.

At four-fifteen, Cynthia urged Katherine to give her a few minutes alone. So much had gone on in the last days and weeks, she said, that she was quite breathless.

"What if you should fall down the stairs?"

Katherine inquired. "And your hair, it's still in curlers!"

Cynthia had known Katherine for just under two hours, but already reckoned her to be a woman who minced no words.

"I'm not going to fall down the stairs," she said. "And the curlers come out in a flash. I must say you look smashing in Olivia's suit, really you do, the color is wonderful on you."

"I've never worn anything this short in my life!" fumed Katherine, peering into the full-length mirror and tugging at her skirt. "I look exactly like Big Bird, I had no *idea* I was so knock-kneed. I'll scandalize the church, your friends will think we're riffraff."

"They'll think no such thing, they've all been dying to meet you." Cynthia urged Katherine toward the door of her bedroom, the bedroom that would, tonight, belong to Walter and Katherine, who currently had no room of their own at all, poor souls.

"I'll take your bouquet out of the parish hall refrigerator," said Katherine, "and see you in the narthex." What could she do with a bride who wanted to be alone? As for herself, she had sprained her ankle twenty minutes before her own wedding and if friends hadn't surrounded her, she might still be lying by the fish pond at that dreadful hotel in the Poconos.

At five 'til five, Father Tim shot his French cuffs and exchanged meaningful glances with Walter and the bishop.

They were cooped into the six-by-eight-foot sacristy like three roosters, he thought, and not a breath of air stirring.

He walked to the door and pushed it open. Avis Packard's cigarette smoke blew in.

" 'Scuse me," said Avis, peering into the sacristy at what he considered a sight for sore eyes. There was their pope, dolled up in a long white robe and the oddest-looking headgear he ever laid eyes on, not to mention that long stick with a curve at the end, which was probably for snatching people up by the neck when they dozed off in the pew. Avis took a deep drag off his filtered Pell Mell and threw it in the bushes.

At precisely five o'clock, Father Tim

heard the organ. What was going on? Why hadn't anyone come to the outer sacristy door to tell them the bride had arrived?

"Don't go out there!" he nearly shouted, as the bishop's hand went for the door that led to the sanctuary. "Walter, please find Katherine, find out what's going on." Somebody had missed a signal, somehow. He felt oddly uneasy.

At five after five, Walter reappeared, looking mystified. "Katherine can't find Cynthia. She was supposed to meet her in the narthex at five 'til."

Ten minutes late! Cynthia Coppersmith was the very soul of punctuality.

He had a gut feeling, and it wasn't good. "I'll be back," he said, sprinting through the open door.

"I'll come with you!" said Walter.

"No! Stay here!"

He dashed up Old Church Lane, cut through Baxter Park, and hit her back steps running.

"Cynthia!" He was trembling as he opened the unlocked door and ran into the hall. He stood for a moment, panting and bewildered, as Violet rubbed against his pant leg. He wished he could find cats more agreeable.

He took the stairs two at a time and hung a left into her bedroom. “Cynthia!”

“Timothy!”

She was beating on her bathroom door from the inside. “Timothy! I can’t get out!”

He spied the blasted doorknob lying on the floor. He picked it up and stuck the stem back in the hole and cranked the knob to the right and the door opened and he saw his bride in her chenile robe and pink curlers, looking agonized.

“Oh, Timothy . . .”

“Don’t talk,” he said. “Don’t even tell me. How can I help you, what can I do?”

She raced to the closet and took out her suit. “I already have my panty hose on, so I’m not starting from scratch. Stand outside and I’ll do my best. Pray for me, darling! Oh, I’m so sorry, I should have borrowed something blue for good luck, what a dreadful mess. . . .”

He stood in the hall and checked his watch. Five-seventeen.

Violet rubbed against his ankle. He felt his jaws beginning to lock.

“OK, you can come in now, I have my suit on, where are my shoes, oh, good grief, how did they get there, I can’t believe this, Timothy, I couldn’t help it, the knob just *fell off,* I yelled out the window and nobody heard, it was awful—"

"Don't talk!" he said, coming into the room. Why was he commanding her not to talk? Let the poor woman talk if she wanted to! Helpless—that's what he felt.

She thumped onto the bench at her dressing table and powdered her face and outlined her lips with a pencil and put on lipstick.

Five-twenty.

Then she did something to her eyebrows and eyelids.

Five-twenty-two.

She sprayed the wisteria scent on her wrists and rubbed them together and touched her wrists to her ears.

He could see Stuart pacing the sacristy, Katherine wringing her hands, Walter going beserk, the entire congregation getting up and walking out, the ham, covered by Saran Wrap, abandoned in the refrigerator. . . .

"Cynthia . . ."

"Oh, dreadful, oh, horrid!" she cried, finishing her mascara with a shaking hand. "And I just remembered, you're not supposed to see the bride before the ceremony!"

"Too late!" he said, eyeing his watch. "Five twenty-four."

"I'm coming, I'm coming!"

She got up and dashed toward him.

"Curlers," he said, his jaws cranking still further into the lock position.

"Rats!"

She plucked curlers from her head like so many feathers from a chicken, and tossed them into the air. They literally rained around the room; he'd never seen anything like it.

"No time to brush!" She looked into the mirror and ran her fingers through her hair. "There! Best I can do. God help me!"

She turned to him now, and he felt a great jolt from heart to spleen. She was so astonishingly beautiful, so radiant, so fresh, it captured his very breath. Thanks be to God, his custard was back. . . .

She grabbed her handbag from the chair. "We can take my car!"

"No place to park!"

"So," she cried, as they headed for the stairs, "race you!"

CHAPTER NINE

The Wedding

In the ninth row of the epistle side, next to the stained-glass window of Christ carrying the lost lamb, Hope Winchester blushed to recall her once-ardent crush on Father Tim. She'd taken every precaution to make certain he knew nothing of it, and now it seemed idiotic to have felt that way about someone twice her age.

She remembered the fluttering of her heart when he came into the bookstore, and all her hard work to learn special words that would intrigue him. She would never admit such a thing to another soul, but she believed herself to be the only person in Mitford who could converse on his level. When she'd learned about Cynthia months ago, she had forced herself to stop thinking such nonsense altogether, and was now truly happy that he and his neighbor had found each other. They seemed perfect together.

Still, on occasion, she missed her old habit of looking for him to pass the shop window and wave, or stop in; and she missed pondering what book she might order that would please and surprise him.

It wasn't that she'd ever wanted to marry him, for heaven's sake, or even be in love with him; it was just that he was so very kind and gentle and made her feel special. Plus he was a lot like herself, deep and sensitive, not to mention a lover of the romantic poets she'd adored since junior high. Early on, she had made it a point to read Wordsworth again, weeping over the Lucy poems, so she could quote passages and dig out morsels to attract his imagination.

"Come in out of the *fretful stir*!" she once said as he popped through the door at Happy Endings.

He had looked up and smiled. "Wordsworth!" he exclaimed, obviously pleased.

How many people would recognize two little words among a poet's thousand? She had felt positively thrilled.

Opening her purse, she examined the contents for the Kleenex she'd stuffed in at the last minute. Though she thought it fatuous to cry at weddings, she deemed it wise to be prepared.

In the fourth row of the epistle side, Gene Bolick wondered what on earth was going on. His watch said five-fifteen. He knew Richard well enough to know he was looking pale after hammering down on the organ all this time with nothing happening.

He glanced again at the bishop's wife, whose head was bowed. Was she praying that the father hadn't chickened out at the last minute? Wouldn't that be a corker if their priest was on a plane bound for the Azores? He didn't know where the Azores were located, but figured it was a distance.

Realizing his fists were clenched and his palms sweaty, he forced his attention to the three-layer orange marmalade sitting in the parish hall refrigerator, looking like a million bucks. He hoped to the Lord the temperature was set right and hadn't accidentally been switched to extra cool, which had once frozen two hundred pimento cheese sandwiches as hard as hockey pucks. He nudged Esther, who appeared to be sleeping under the brim of the hat she wore only to weddings and funerals.

Esther was not sleeping, she was thinking, and ignored the nudge. Didn't she deserve to sit and catch her breath until these people got their act together and got on with it? She was thinking that maybe she'd put in too much sugar, she knew Father Tim didn't like too much sugar, but why, after all these years and hundreds of cakes later, did she still worry and fret over her work as if she'd never baked a cake in her life? The Expert is what some called her, but who could feel like an expert at something as willful and fickle as a cake, cakes having, as she'd always feared, a mind of their own? Use the same ingredients in the same amounts, time after time after time, and were her cakes ever the same? Not as far as she could see.

She'd always depended on Gene to be the judge and he hadn't failed her yet. Gene would take a taste of the batter and his eyes would wander around the room, as if that little taste had transported him on some round of roving thoughts and idle speculation. After a while, he'd come back to himself. "Best yet!" he might say, or, "Couldn't be better!"

Whatever he said, he would have reasoned it out, thought it through, and she could depend on the answer—which was more than most wives could say of their husbands. Now, you take Father Tim, his wife would be able to depend on him—the only question was, was she deserving of such a prize? She thought she was, she hoped she was; she was crazy about Cynthia, but hadn't her senator husband, or was he a congressman, run around with other women? What did that mean? Cynthia didn't look like a cold fish—the opposite, more like it.

Anyway, didn't their rector have enough sense to come in out of the rain and choose who he wanted to spend the rest of his life with? And in the last few months, hadn't she and everybody else in the parish heard him laugh and joke like never before?

Lord help, it must be virgin's bower that was making her eyes burn and her sinuses drain. Virgin's bower mixed with lilies, the bane of her existence, and nobody with the simple courtesy to remove the pollen from the anthers, which means it would be flying around in here like so much snuff, and her with no Sinu-Tabs in her pocketbook and too late to do anything about it.

Pete Jamison made his way into the nave of Lord's chapel, where a robed and expectant choir overflowed from the narthex.

Embarrassed at being late, he dodged through the throng to the rear wall and stood, reverent and shaken, feeling at once a stranger here and also oddly at home. He realized his breath was coming in shallow gasps, probably because he'd run more than a block from the Collar Button where he'd parked—or was it from the excitement he felt in being here for the first time since his life had been changed forever?

Two rows from the front, on the gospel side, Miss Sadie sat holding hands with Louella, oblivious of the time and enjoying the music. She felt certain that the emotions stirring in her breast were those of any proud mother.

After all, Father Tim wasn't merely her priest, her brother in Christ, and one of the dearest friends of this life, he was also like a son. Who else would run up the hill after a hard rain and empty the soup kettle sitting brimful under the leak in her ceiling? And who else would sit for hours listening to her ramble, while appearing to be genuinely interested? God in His Providence had not seen fit to bless her with children, but He'd given her Olivia Harper and Timothy Kavanagh! And, since she'd helped raise Louella from a baby, she could almost count her pewmate as her child—Lord knows, she wasn't but ten years old when she'd begun diapering and dressing that little dark baby as if it were her own!

Miss Sadie wiped a tear with the handkerchief she had carefully chosen for the occasion, a lace-trimmed square of white Irish linen monogrammed with her mother's initial, and turned and smiled proudly at Louella, who looked a perfect blossom in the lavender dress.

Dooley Barlowe swallowed hard. It would have been fine if everything had started when it was supposed to, but here it was twenty minutes after five and who knew where Cynthia and Father Tim were, like maybe they both got scared and ran off, or had a fight and weren't going through with it. He felt foolish sitting here in the front row, all of them tricked into waiting like a bunch of stupid goats, listening to organ music. He was about to die to go to the toilet, but if he tried now to make it to the parish hall, everybody would know where he was going.

He crossed his legs and squeezed his eyes shut and jiggled his foot and went through the verses again.

Reverend Absalom Greer had purposely

followed Sadie Eleanor Baxter into the nave, though he tried to appear as if he had no idea she was anywhere around. He followed her so he could sit behind her and look at her again. Who knows when the Lord might call him Home and this would be his last chance on earth to see her face?

The way it fell out was, he was the first to go into the pew behind her, which meant he had to sit all the way to the end, by the window of Jesus washing the disciples' feet. He thought this location was a blessing from above, seeing as he could look at her in profile instead of at the little gray knot on the back of her head.

Absalom felt such a stirring in his breast that he might have been fourteen years old, going up Hogback to see Annie Hawkins, carrying two shot quails and a mess of turnips in a poke. Annie's mama was dead of pneumonia and her daddy not heard of since the flood, and as Annie was left to raise a passel of brothers and sisters, he never went up Hogback without victuals; once he'd killed a deer and helped her skin it and jerk the meat.

It had taken him three years to get over big-boned, sassy-mouthed Annie Hawkins, but he'd never gotten over Sadie Baxter.

Sadie had filled his dreams, his waking hours, his prayers for many a year; he'd earnestly hoped she would forget Willard Porter and marry him. Finally, the burning hope had fizzled into a kind of faint glow that laid on his heart like embers, making him smile occasionally and nod his head and whisper her name. He'd confessed this lingering and soulful love only to the Almighty and never told another, though sometimes his sister, Lottie, suspicioned how he was feeling and derided him with a cool stare.

Reverend Greer settled stiffly into the creaking pew and nodded to those around him and bowed his head and prayed for his dear brother in the Lord, Tim Kavanagh, as fine a man as God ever gave breath to, amen. When he lifted his head and looked at Sadie's profile and the tender smile on her face, the tears sprang instantly to his eyes and he fetched the handkerchief from his pocket, the handkerchief Lottie had starched and ironed 'til it crackled like paper, and thanked the Lord Jesus that he still had eyes to see and tears to wipe, hallelujah.

Pete Jamison, though six-foot-three, eased himself up on the balls of his feet so he could see down front to the gospel side. He found the pew where he sat the day he had wandered, alarmed and desperate, into the darkened church. It had been sometime around Thanksgiving and there was snow on the ground; he remembered noticing his incoming tracks as he left the church a different man, one to whom everything seemed fresh and new.

He'd knelt that day and cried out to God, asking a simple question: *Are you up there?* He wasn't trying to get anything from God, he wasn't begging for money or success, though at the time he urgently needed both, he just wanted to know more desperately than he'd ever wanted to know anything in his life, if God was up there—no more ifs, ands, or buts, just *yes or no.* Now he knew the answer more completely than he could ever have hoped or imagined.

He felt tears smart his eyes, and his heart expand. The music was beginning to enter him; he was beginning to hear it over the pounding of his heart, and was glad to feel the joy of this time and place as if it might, in some small way, belong also to him.

Standing outside the church door in the warm September afternoon, Katherine Kavanagh saw the bride and groom literally galloping down the street, and suppressed a shout of relief. She tugged on her skirt for the umpteenth time and tried to relax her tense shoulders so the jacket would fall below her waistline. In the desperate half hour she'd waited for Cynthia to show up, she had decided what to do. The minute she returned home, she was suing the airline, who had gotten away with their criminal behavior long enough.

Though wanting very much to dash across the churchyard and meet Cynthia, she realized this impetuous behavior would cause her skirt to ride up. She stood, therefore, frozen as a mullet as she watched the bride sprinting into the home stretch.

Next to the aisle on the epistle side, Emma Newland nearly jumped out of her seat as the organ cranked up to a mighty roar. The thirty-seven-voice ecumenical choir was at last processing in, sending a blast of energy through the congregation as if someone had fired a cannon.

The congregation shot to its feet, joining the choir in singing hymn number 410 with great abandon and unmitigated relief:

Praise my Soul the King of Heaven;
To His feet thy tribute bring;

Ransomed, healed, restored, forgiven,
Evermore His praises sing;
Alleluia, alleluia!
Praise the everlasting King!

Dooley Barlowe felt something happen to the top of his head. He had opened his mouth with the rest of the congregation and heard words flow out in a strong and steady voice he scarcely recognized as his own.

Praise Him for His grace and favor;
To His people in distress;
Praise Him still the same as ever,
Slow to chide and swift to bless.
Alleluia, alleluia,
Glorious in His faithfulness.

Dooley thought Father's Tim's voice carried loud and clear from where he stood with the bishop and Walter at the rail. The bishop was decked out in a really weird hat, but looked cool as anything otherwise. As for Father Tim, he'd never seen him in a tuxedo before and thought he looked . . . *different,* maybe sort of handsome.

The tremor in his stomach subsided; he felt suddenly tall and victorious and forgot about having to go to the toilet.

Hessie Mayhew gazed at Stuart Cullen, whom she found exceedingly good-looking, and thought it was a darned good thing that Episcopal clergy were allowed to marry, otherwise it could cause a rumpus. She'd never chased after clergy like some women she knew, but she couldn't dismiss their powerful attraction, either. Anyway, who'd want to tie the knot with a preacher and end up with a whole churchful of people pulling you to pieces day and night? *Head this, chair that!* No, indeed, no clergy for her, thank you very much.

She fluffed her scarf over the odd rash that had appeared on her neck, dismissing it as one of the several hazards of her calling, and hoped the bishop was noticing the flowers and that someone would tell him about Hessie Mayhew, who, even if she was Presbyterian, knew a thing or two about the right and proper way to beautify a church.

Angels, help us to adore Him;
Ye behold Him face to face;
Sun and moon, bow down before Him,

Dwellers in all time and space.
Alleluia, alleluia!
Praise with us the God of grace.

Jena Ivey could not carry a tune in a bucket and preferred to look at the stained-glass window for the duration of the processional hymn. The window was of Christ being baptized while John the Baptist stood onshore in his animal skin outfit. It seemed to her that St. John could have presented himself better, seeing it was the Lord Jesus who was getting baptized; like it wasn't as if St. John didn't know He was coming, for Pete's sake. Look at the three wise men, who always appeared nicely groomed, though they'd been riding camels for *two years*.

She was startled by the sound of the trumpet only a few feet away, causing, simultaneously, an outbreak of goose bumps and a wild pounding of her heart.

Then, suddenly, there was the matron of honor charging down the aisle; Jena didn't have a clue who this woman might be, she was tall as a giraffe. That's the way it was with weddings, they turned out people you'd never seen before in your life and would never see again.

Emma thought the matron of honor blew past like she was going to a fire, canceling any opportunity to study the skimpy cut of Katherine Kavanagh's suit, or to check out the kind of shoes she had on. She did, however, get a whiff of something that wasn't flowers, it was definitely perfume, possibly from Macy's or some such.

Then came Rebecca Jane Owen and Amy Larkin, wearing velvet hair bows the color of green Baxter apples. As far as Emma could tell, they were fairly smothered with flowers; you'd think Hessie Mayhew would scale down for children, but oh, no, Hessie scaled up, these two infants were fairly tottering under the weight of what looked like full bushes of hydrangeas.

Jabbing Harold to do the same, Emma swiveled her head to see the bride trotting behind the small entourage.

Cynthia Coppersmith was flushed as a girl—her eyes shining, her face expectant, her hair curled damply around her face as if she'd just won a game of tag. Emma thought she looked sixteen years old if she was a day, and her suit was exactly the color of a crayon Emma had favored in first grade, aquamarine. She appeared to be moving fast, but that was all right—hadn't she herself run lickety-split to marry Harold Newland, starved to death for affection after ten years of widowhood and thrilled at the prospect of someone to hug her neck every night?

Emma leaned over the arm of the pew so she could see Father Tim as his bride approached the altar. The look on his face made her want to shut her eyes, as if she'd intruded upon something terribly precious and private.

"Dearly beloved, we have come together in the presence of God to witness and bless the joining together of this man and this woman in Holy Matrimony. The bond and covenant of marriage was established by God in creation, and our Lord Jesus Christ adorned this manner of life by His presence and first miracle at a wedding in Cana of Galilee. It signifies to us the mystery of the union between Christ and His Church, and Holy Scripture commends it to be honored among all people.

"The union of husband and wife in heart, body, and mind is intended by God for their mutual joy; for the help and comfort given one another in prosperity and adversity; and, when it is God's will, for the procreation of children and their nurture in the knowledge and love of the Lord. Therefore marriage is not to be entered into unadvisedly or lightly, but reverently, deliberately, and in accordance with the purposes for which it was instituted by God.

"Into this holy union, Cynthia Clary Coppersmith and Timothy Andrew Kavanagh now come to be joined. . . ."

Uncle Billy Watson hoped and prayed his wife would not fall asleep and snore; it was all he could do to keep his own eyes open. Sitting with so many people in a close church on a close afternoon was nearabout more than a man could handle. He kept alert by asking himself a simple question: When it came time, would he have mustard on his ham, or eat it plain?

"Cynthia, will you have this man to be your husband; to live together in the covenant of marriage? Will you love him, comfort him, honor and keep him, in sickness and in health; and, forsaking all others, be faithful to him as long as you both shall live?"

Winnie Ivey clasped her hand over her heart and felttears burn her cheeks. To think that God would give this joy to people as old as herself and no spring chickens . . .

The bride's vow was heard clearly throughout the nave. "I will!"

"Timothy, will you have this woman to be your wife; to live together in the covenant of marriage? Will you love her, comfort her, honor and keep her, in sickness and in health; and, forsaking all others, be faithful to her as long as you both shall live?"

"I will!"

"Will all of you witnessing these promises do all in your power to uphold these two persons in their marriage?"

"We will!"

At the congregational response, Dooley Barlowe quickly left the front pew by the sacristy door and took his place in front of the altar rail. As he faced the cross and bowed, one knee trembled slightly, but he locked it in place and drew a deep breath.

Don't let me mess up, he prayed, then opened his mouth and began to sing.

Oh, perfect Love, all human thought
transcending,
Lowly we kneel in prayer before Thy
throne,
That theirs may be the love which knows
no ending,
Whom Thou forevermore dost join in one.

It all sounded lovey-dovey, thought Emma, but she knew one thing—it would never work if Cynthia sat around drawing cats while her husband wanted his dinner! Oh, Lord, she was doing it again, and this time without intending to; she was running down a person who didn't have a mean bone in her body. She closed her eyes and asked forgiveness.

She'd held on to her reservations about Cynthia like a tightwad squeezes a dollar, but she felt something in her heart finally giving way as if floodgates were opening, and she knew at last that she honestly approved of the union that would bind her priest's heart for all eternity. Disgusted with herself for having forgotten to bring a proper handkerchief, Emma mopped her eyes with a balled-up napkin from Pizza Hut.

Oh, perfect Life, be Thou their full
assurance
Of tender charity and steadfast faith,
Of patient hope and quiet, brave
endurance,
With childlike trust that fears nor pain
nor death.

Pete Jamison pondered the words "child-like trust that fears nor pain nor death," and knew that's what he'd been given the day he'd cried out to God in this place and God had answered by sending Father Kavanagh. He remembered distinctly what the father had said: "You may be asking the wrong question. What you may want to ask is, Are You down here?"

He'd prayed a prayer that day with the father, a simple thing, and was transformed forever, able now to stand in this place knowing without any doubt at all that, yes, God is down here and faithfully with us. He remembered the prayer as if he'd uttered it only yesterday. *Thank you, God, for loving me, and for sending Your son to die for my sins. I sincerely repent of my sins, and receive Christ as my personal savior. Now, as Your child, I turn my entire life over to You.* He'd never been one to surrender anything, yet that day, he had surrendered everything. When the church was quiet and the celebration over, he'd go down front and kneel in the same place he'd knelt before, and give thanks.

Gene Bolick wondered how a man Father Tim's age would be able to keep up his husbandly duties. As for himself, all he wanted to do at night was hit his recliner after supper and sleep 'til bedtime. Maybe the father knew something he didn't know. . . .

Louella heard people all around her sniffling and blowing their noses, it was a regular free-for-all. And Miss Sadie, she was the worst of the whole kaboodle, bawling into her mama's handkerchief to beat the band. Miss Sadie loved that little redheaded, freckle-face white boy because he reminded her of Willard Porter, who came up hard like Dooley and ended up amounting to something.

Louella thought Miss Cynthia looked beautiful in her dressy suit; and that little bit of shimmering thread in the fabric and those jeweled buttons, now, that was something, that was nice, and look there, she wasn't wearing shoes dyed to match, she was wearing black pumps as smart as you please. Louella knew from reading the magazines Miss Olivia brought to Fernbank that shoes dyed to match were out of style

It seemed to her that the sniffling was getting worse by the minute, and no wonder—just *listen* to that boy sing! Louella settled back in the pew, personally proud of Dooley, Miss Cynthia, the father, and the whole shooting match.

Finally deciding on mustard, Uncle Billy abandoned the game. He'd better come up with another way to noodle his noggin or he'd drop off in a sleep so deep they'd have to knock him upside the head with a two-by-four. He determined to mentally practice his main joke, and if that didn't work, he was done for.

Grant them the joy which brightens
earthly sorrow,
Grant them the peace which calms all
earthly strife,
And to life's day the glorious unknown
morrow
That dawns upon eternal love and life.
Amen.

Dooley returned to his pew without feeling the floor beneath his feet. He was surprised to find he was trembling, as if he'd been live-wired. But it wasn't fear, anymore, it was . . . something else.

Father Tim took Cynthia's right hand in his, and carefully spoke the words he had never imagined might be his own.

"In the name of God, I, Timothy, take you, Cynthia, to be my wife, to have and to hold from this day forward, for better for worse, for richer for poorer, in sickness and in health, to love and to cherish, until we are parted by death.

"This is my solemn vow."

They loosed their hands for a moment, a slight movement that caused the candle flames on the altar to tremble. Then she took his right hand in hers.

"In the name of God, I, Cynthia, take you, Timothy, to be my husband, to have and to hold from this day forward, for better for worse, for richer for poorer, in sickness and in health, to love and to cherish, until we are parted by death.

"This is my solemn vow."

As Walter presented the ring to the groom, the bishop raised his right hand. "Bless, O Lord, these rings to be a sign of the vows by which this man and this woman have bound themselves to each other; through Jesus Christ our Lord, Amen."

"Cynthia, I give you this ring as a symbol of my vow, and with all that I am, and all that I have, I honor you, in the name of the Father, and of the Son, and of the Holy Spirit."

She felt the worn gold ring slipping on her finger; it seemed weightless, a band of silk.

Katherine stepped forward then, delivering the heavy gold band with the minuscule engraving upon its inner circle: *Until heaven and then forever.*

"Timothy . . . I give you this ring as a symbol of my vow, and with all that I am, and all that I have, I honor you, in the name of the Father, and of the Son, and of the Holy Spirit."

Hessie Mahew was convinced the bishop looked right into her eyes as he spoke.

"Now that Cynthia and Timothy have given themselves to each other by solemn vows, with the joining of hands and the giving and receiving of rings, I pronounce that they are husband and wife, in the name of the Father, and of the Son, and of the Holy Spirit.

"Those whom God has joined together . . . let no man put asunder."

Dooley felt the lingering warmth in his face and ears, and heard the pounding of his heart. No, it wasn't fear anymore, it was something else, and he thought he knew what it was.

It was something maybe like . . . happiness.

CHAPTER TEN

The Beginning

Henry Oldman met them at the airport in the Cullen camp car, a 1981 turquoise Chevy Impala that made the rector's Buick look mint condition, showroom.

It was theirs to drive for the week, and they dropped Henry off at his trim cottage with a two-stall cow barn and half-acre garden plot. While Cynthia chatted with Mrs. Oldman, Henry gave him the drill.

"New tires," Henry said, delivering a swift kick to the aforesaid.

"Wonderful!"

"New fan belt."

"Great!"

"Miz Oldman washed y'r seat covers."

"Outstanding. Glad to hear it."

"Mildew."

The handyman who'd served the Cullens for nearly fifty Maine summers was sizing him up pretty good, he thought; trying to figure whether he'd be a proper steward for such fine amenities.

"You'll be stayin' in th' big house, what they call th' lodge. Miz Oldman put this 'n' that in y'r icebox. Juice an' cereal an' what-not."

"We thank you."

Henry pulled at his lower lip. "Washin' machine door come off, wouldn't use it much if I was you."

"I suppose not."

"Downstairs toilet handle needs jigglin' or it's bad to run. Ordered th' part t' fix it, but hadn't got it yet."

"We'll remember."

"You got a pretty big hole in y'r floor. Last year or two, we've had more'n one snake come in."

"*Which* floor exactly?"

"Dinin' room. I set a barrel over it, Bishop said it'd be all right 'til I can get somethin' to fix it. Had a rag in th' hole but somethin' chewed it out."

Now we're getting down to it, he thought.

"Got rid of y'r ants, but not much luck with th' mice, mice're smarter'n we give 'em credit for."

His wife didn't need to know this. Not any of this.

Henry kicked the tire again for good measure. "Attic stairs, you pull 'em down, they won't go up ag'in."

The rector shrugged. He'd rather have a root canal without Novocain than stand here another minute.

"Course you know there's no electric at th' Cullen place."

No electric? His blood pressure was shooting up; he could feel the pounding in his temples. "What *lights* the place? *Pine torches?*"

"Only two places hereabout still has gaslit."

He hadn't fared so badly since trucking off at the age of nine to Camp Mulhaven, where he entertained a double-barreled dose of chiggers and poison ivy. What would Cynthia think? What had he gotten them into? He'd wring his bishop's neck, the old buzzard; his so-called honeymoon cottage was a blasted tumbledown shack! He'd call the moment they arrived and give Stuart Cullen a generous piece of his mind. . . .

"Wouldn't keep any food settin' on th' porch." Henry removed a toothpick from his shirt pocket and pried the circumference of his left molar.

"Why's that?" He couldn't remember ever leaving food on a porch. Why would anyone leave food on a porch?

"Bear."

Bear?

He craned his neck to peer at his wife, standing with Mrs. Oldman by a flower bed. Thank heaven she hadn't overheard the last pronouncement.

"Well!" said the rector, putting an end to the veritable Niagara of bad news. "We'll see you out when we bring the car back."

"You'll see me tomorrow," said Henry. "Bishop called today, asked me to come check th' water, see if it's runnin' muddy. Bishop's daddy, he tried to dig a new well before he passed, but . . ." Henry raised both hands as if he had no responsibility for the failure of this mission, it was some bitter destiny over which he'd lacked any control. "Bishop said bring you some speckled trout, you know how to clean trout?"

"Ahhh," he said, wordless. He'd never cleaned trout in his life.

Henry raised an eyebrow. "I'll have Miz Oldman do it for you."

He could hardly wait to get in the car, if only to sit down.

These were the days of heaven. . . .

He walked out to the porch, loving the feel of old wood, silken with wear, under his bare feet.

The view took his breath away. Early morning mist hovered above the platinum lake, and just there, near its center, a small island with a cabin on its narrow shore. . . .

Nothing stirred except waterfowl: He saw a merganser and a string of young ply the water with great determination. Next to the lodge, cedar waxwings dived and swooped in the seed-dowered garden.

It would definitely take some getting used to, but he was liking this place better with every passing moment.

He expanded his chest and sucked in his stomach and circled his arms like propellers, awash in happiness, in contentment—in a kind of energized sloth, if there could be such a thing.

Though they'd slept at his house the first night and at hers on the second, last night had somehow marked the true beginning.

At the rectory, his antediluvian mattress had rolled them into the middle of the bed like hotdogs in a bun. At her house, circumstances were considerably improved, though the alarm clock had, oddly, gone off at three a.m. Odder still, the clock wasn't in its usual place on her bedside table. Failing to turn on a lamp, they leapt up to locate the blasted thing and, navigating by moonlight alone, had crashed into each other at the bookcase.

But last night had been everything, everything and more.

He cupped his hands and drew them to his face and smelled her warm scent, now and forever mingled with his own. In truth, he had entered into a realm that had little to do with familiar reason and everything to do with a power and mystery he'd never believed possible. Perhaps for the first time in his life, there was nothing he craved to possess, nothing he felt lacking; he was only waiting for his coffee to perk.

He had schlepped the coffee in his suitcase, for which effort his underwear smelled of decaf Antigua and his socks of full-bore French Roast. Eager to begin their honeymoon on a note of thoughtfulness, if not downright servitude, he had gone to the kitchen to concoct the coffee, to be followed by a breakfast of . . . he opened the cabinets and checked the inventory . . . a breakfast of raisin bran in blue tin bowls.

He'd never messed with gas stoves. While chefs were commonly known to prefer cooking with gas, he'd always feared it might blow his head off. Dangerous stuff, gas, he could smell it in here more strongly than in the rest of the house. If he lit a match, they could be spending their honeymoon in Quebec. . . .

But come on, for Pete's sake, wasn't he up for a little excitement on this incredibly beautiful, endlessly promising day? Wasn't all of this an adventure, a new beginning?

He withdrew a kitchen match from the box and studied it soberly, then walked to the gas-powered refrigerator and retrieved the coffee. Now. Where might the coffee pot be lurking?

Aha. That must be it on the shelf above the stove. Then again, surely not. He took it down and inspected it. Campfires. Many campfires. He lifted the lid. Oh, yes, just like his mother once used, there was the basket on its stick. . . .

Thinking he should try and clean the pot, he removed the basket and peered inside.

Hopeless! He rinsed it out under a trickle of cold water. That would have to do; this was not, after all, a military kitchen.

He filled the basket with some satisfaction, thankful he'd brought preground, otherwise they'd be chewing beans. . . .

His wife appeared, looking touseled and teenaged in her nightgown. She slipped her arms around his waist and kissed him. "I love campfire coffee!"

Using the flat of his hand, he hammered down on the lid, which, once round, had somehow become oval with age. "What don't you love, Kavanagh?"

"Ducks that cry all night, beds with creaking springs, and feather pillows with little gnawing things inside."

"My sentiments exactly." He smiled at his bride, set the pot on the stove, and struck the match.

"Stand back!" he warned.

"Those weren't ducks calling last night."

They were rocking on the porch, side by side. He had never felt so far from a vestry in his life. "They're loons."

"Loons!" she said, marveling.

The ensuing silence was punctuated with birdsong.

"Related to the auks."

"Who, dearest? The Cullens?"

"The loons."

"Of course."

"They mate for life."

"Lovely! Just like us."

They watched the navigation of yet another duck family, thought they spotted a bald eagle, counted three kingfishers, sipped a second cup of coffee.

He relished their easy quietude this morning; it held a richness to be savored. Surely he was blessed beyond all reckoning to have a highly verbal wife who could also be quiet. He had always valued that in a woman, in a man, in a friend. Though his mother had possessed a sparkling way with people and was bright and eager in conversation on many subjects, she also had a gentle quietude that made her companionship ever agreeable.

"God is mercifully allowing me to forget the dreadful experience of getting here," Cynthia said of yesterday's journey.

"You mean the four-hour mechanical delay, the two-hour layover, and the forty-five minutes on the runway with no air stirring in the cabin?"

"The same!" she said.

"The usual," he said.

He wondered what his dog might be doing at the moment. And how about his boy—how was he faring? He'd call home tonight. On second thought, he could forget calling anybody. His bishop had conveniently forgotten to say there was no phone at Cullen camp.

"I love this place, Timothy. It's so wonderfully simple."

"What would you like to do today?"

"Nothing!"

He was thrilled to hear it.

"Of course," she said, "we might pop down to the village and peek in the shops."

He hated to be the bearer of bad news. "Umm . . ."

"There are no shops!" she said, reading his mind.

"Right. Only a service station, a small grocery store with a post office, and an unused church."

"So we can poke through the graveyard. I love graveyards!"

He grinned. "Of course you love graveyards. But I don't think there's a graveyard at this particular church. Stuart mentioned that the flock was buried elsewhere."

She leaned back in the rocker and turned her head and looked into his eyes, smiling. "Well, then," she murmured.

He took her hand and lightly kissed the tips of her fingers. "Well, then," he said.

Henry had come on Wednesday with fresh trout and a blackberry pie baked by Mrs. Oldman, and on Thursday with a free-range chicken, a quart of green beans, a sack of beets and potatoes, and a providential lump of home-churned butter.

In truth, they were savoring unforgettable meals at an oilcloth-covered table on the porch, lighted in the evening by a kerosene lantern. One evening had been crisp and cold enough for a fire; they'd hauled the table indoors and dined by the hearth on a hearty vegetable stew, sopping their bowls with bread toasted over the fire and slathered with Oldman butter. Each dish they prepared was such a stunning success that he now dreaded going home to four pathetic electric eyes, albeit on a range of more recent vintage.

In the four days since arriving, they'd clung to the porch like moss to a log, celebrating the sunrise, cheering the dazzling sunsets. Their off-porch expeditions had been few—a walk around the lake, twice, and a canoe excursion to the island. Not being water lovers, they made the island foray with considerable temerity. Finding the cabin empty, they picnicked under a fir tree on a threadbare Indian blanket and, setting off for home, found the trip across had so bolstered their confidence that they paddled north for a couple of miles, only to be drenched by a downpour.

Yesterday, they'd climbed through the window of another cabin in the Cullen camp. Sitting on the floor of a room built in 1917, according to the date carved on a rafter, they drank Earl Grey tea from a thermos and told all the jokes they could remember from childhood.

Finding themselves on a roll, she suggested they draw broomstraws to see who'd entertain the other with a retelling of Uncle Billy's wedding joke.

The rector was not pleased to draw the short straw. After all, who but Uncle Billy could tell an Uncle Billy joke? He returned the straw. "Sorry," he said, "but this joke can't be done without a cane."

She got up and went to the fireplace,

whipped the broom off the hearth, and handed it over.

"Is there no balm . . . ?" he sighed.

"None!" she said.

Using the hearth for a stage and the broom for a cane, he hunkered down and clasped his right lower back, where he thought he might actually feel an arthritic twinge.

"Wellsir, two fellers was workin' together, don't you know. First'n, he was bright 'n cheerful, th' other'n, he didn't have nothin' to say, seem like he was mad as whiz. First'n said, 'Did you wake up grouchy this mornin'?' Other'n said, 'Nossir, I let 'er wake 'er own self up.' "

Hoots, cheers, general merriment.

"That's just m' warm-up, don't you know, hit ain't m' main joke."

The audience settled down and gazed at him raptly.

"Wellsir, Ol' Adam, he was mopin' 'round th' Garden of Eden feelin' lonesome, don't you know. So, the Lord asked 'im, said, 'Adam, what's ailin' you?' Adam said he didn't have nobody t' talk to. Wellsir, th' Lord tol' 'im He'd make somebody t' keep 'im comp'ny, said hit'd be a woman, said, 'This woman'll rustle up y'r grub an' cook it f'r you, an' when you go t' wearin' clothes, she'll wash 'em f'r you, an' when you make a decision on somethin', she'll agree to it.' Said, 'She'll not nag n'r torment you a single time, an' when you have a fuss, she'll give you a big hug an' say you was right all along.'

"Ol' Adam, he was jist a-marvelin' at this.

"The Lord went on, said, 'She'll never complain of a headache, an' 'll give you love an' passion whenever you call for it, an' when you have young'uns, she'll not ask y' to git up in th' middle of th' night.' Adam's eyes got real big, don't you know, said 'What'll a woman like 'at *cost* a feller?' Th' Lord said, 'A arm an' a leg!'

"Adam pondered a good bit, said, 'What d'you reckon I could git f'r a rib?' "

Generous applause, ending with the whistle his wife learned as a ten-year-old marble player.

Crawling out the way they'd come in, they left the cabin before dusk and trekked to the lodge on an overgrown path.

During these jaunts, he faithfully looked for bear and stayed alert to protect his wife, though he saw nothing more suspicious than a raccoon seeking to purloin Wednesday's chicken bones.

Today, Cynthia had hauled out sketch

pads and pencils and abandoned any notion of leaving the porch. She vowed she'd seen a moose swimming in the lake and was not keen to miss further sightings. He, meanwhile, lay in a decrepit hammock and read G. K. Chesterton.

Peace covered them like a shawl; he couldn't remember such a time of prolonged ease. There were, however, moments when Guilt snatched him by the scruff of the neck, determined to persuade him this was a gift he had no right to unwrap and enjoy, and he'd better watch his step or *else*. . . .

"Listen to this," he said. " 'An adventure is only an inconvenience rightly considered. An inconvenience is only an adventure wrongly considered.' "

She laughed. "I didn't know G.K. had been to Cullen camp."

"And this: 'The Christian ideal has not been tried and found wanting. It has been found difficult, and left untried.' Does that nail it on the *head*?" He fairly whooped.

"I love seeing you like this," she said.

"Like what?"

"Happy . . . resting . . . at ease. No evening news, no phones, no one pulling you this way and that."

"Stuart knew what he was doing, after all."

"I have a whole new respect for your bishop," she declared.

A loon called, a dragonfly zoomed by the porch rail.

"I heard something in our room last night," she said. "Something *skittering* across the floor. What do you think it was?"

"Oh, I don't know—maybe a chipmunk?" Right there was proof positive that his brain was still working.

"I love chipmunks!"

He put the Chesterton on the floor beside the hammock and lay dazed and dreaming, complete. "'Blessed be the Lord . . . ,'" he murmured.

"'. . . who daily loadeth us with benefits!'" she exclaimed, finishing the verse from Psalm Sixty-eight.

A wife who could read his mind and finish his Scripture verses. Amazing. . . .

When he awoke, he heard only the faint whisper of her pencils on paper.

"Dearest, could you please zip to the store for us?"

"That car will not *zip* anywhere," he said.

"Yes, but we can't go on like two chicks

in the nest, with poor Henry our mother hen. We must have *supplies*."

"I suppose it would be a good thing to keep the battery charged."

"A quart of two-percent milk," she said, without looking up from her sketch pad, "whole wheat English muffins, brown eggs, an onion—we can't make another meal without an onion—and three lemons—"

"Wait!" He hauled himself over the side of the creaking hammock and trotted into the house for a pen and paper.

She held up the sketch and squinted at it. "Oh, and some grapes!" she called after him. "And bacon! Wouldn't it be lovely to smell bacon frying in the morning? I do love raisin bran, Timothy, but *really*. . . ."

Though the late afternoon temperature felt unseasonably warm when he left the car, it was refreshingly cool as he entered the darkened store.

A man in a green apron was dumping potatoes from a sack into a bin; he looked up and nodded.

The rector nodded back, wondering at

his odd sense of liberty in being untethered, yet wondering still more about his desire to hurry back to his wife. This was, after all, the first time they'd been apart since the wedding; he felt . . . barren, somehow, *bereft*. Perhaps it was the sixtysomething years for which, without knowing it, his soul had waited for this inexpressible joy, and he didn't want to miss a single moment of it. Then again, his joy might owe nothing to having waited, and everything to love, and love alone.

He didn't understand these things, perhaps he never would; all he knew or understood was that he wanted to inhale her, to wear her under his very skin—God's concept of "one flesh" had sprung to life for him in an extraordinary way, it was food, it was nectar; their love seemed the hope of the world, somehow. . . .

He chose a package of thick-sliced market bacon. This was living on the edge, and no two ways about it.

But perhaps he was happiest, in reflection, about the other waiting, the times when the temptation to have it all had been nearly unbearable, but they had drawn back, obeying God's wisdom for their lives. The drawing back had shaken him, yes, and shaken her, for their love had exposed their desire in a way they'd never known before. Yet, His grace had made them able to wait, to concentrate on the approaching feast instead of the present hunger.

He set his basket on the counter.

"You over on the lake?" the man asked.

"We are."

"Looks like you'll have a fine sunset this evenin'."

He peered through the store windows toward the tree line. *Holy smoke!* If he hurried, he could make it back to the lodge in time. . . .

"Anything else I can round up for you?"

"This will do it."

"You sure, now?"

As he took out his wallet, he realized he couldn't stop smiling.

"Thank you, this is all," he said. "I have absolutely everything."